Preface to Androcles and the Lion

George Bernard Shaw

Contents

PREFACE TO ANDROCLES AND THE LION

BY

George Bernard Shaw

PREFACE ON THE PROSPECTS OF CHRISTIANITY

WHY NOT GIVE CHRISTIANITY A TRIAL?

The question seems a hopeless one after 2000 years of resolute adherence to the old cry of "Not this man, but Barabbas." Yet it is beginning to look as if Barabbas was a failure, in spite of his strong right hand, his victories, his empires, his millions of money, and his moralities and churches and political constitutions. "This man" has not been a failure yet; for nobody has ever been sane enough to try his way. But he has had one quaint triumph. Barabbas has stolen his name and taken his cross as a standard. There is a sort of compliment in that. There is even a sort of loyalty in it, like that of the brigand who breaks every law and yet claims to be a patriotic subject of the king who makes them. We have always had a curious feeling that though we crucified Christ on a stick, he somehow managed to get hold of the right end of it, and that if we were better men we might try his plan. There have been one or two grotesque attempts at it by inadequate people, such as the Kingdom of God in Munster, which was ended by crucifixion so much more atrocious than the one on Calvary that the bishop who took the part of Annas went home and died of horror. But responsible people have never made such attempts. The moneyed, respectable, capable world has been steadily anti-Christian and Barabbasque since the crucifixion; and the specific doctrine of Jesus has not in all that time been put into political or general social practice. I am no more a Christian than Pilate was, or you, gentle reader; and yet, like Pilate, I greatly prefer Jesus to Annas and Caiaphas; and I am ready to admit that after contemplating the world and human nature for nearly sixty years, I see no way out of the world's misery but the way which would have been found by Christ's will if he had undertaken the work of a modern practical statesman. Pray do not at this early point lose patience with me and shut the book. I assure you I am as sceptical and scientific and modern a thinker as you will find anywhere. I grant you I know a great deal more about economics and politics than Jesus did, and can do things he could not do. I am by all Barabbasque standards a person of much better character and standing, and greater practical sense. I have no sympathy with vagabonds and talkers who try to reform society by taking men away from their regular productive work and making vagabonds and talkers of them too; and if I had been Pilate I should have recognized as plainly as he the necessity for suppressing attacks on the existing social order, however corrupt that order might be, by people with no knowledge of government and no power to construct political machinery to carry out their views, acting on the very dangerous delusion that the end of the world was at hand. I make no defence of such Christians as Savonarola and John of Leyden: they were scuttling the ship before they had learned how to build a raft; and it became necessary to throw them overboard to save the crew. I say this to set myself right with respectable society; but I must still insist that if Jesus could have worked out the practical problems of a Communist constitution, an admitted obligation to deal with crime without revenge or punishment, and a full assumption by humanity of divine responsibilities, he would have conferred an incalculable benefit on mankind, because these distinctive demands of his are now turning out to be good sense and sound economics.

I say distinctive, because his common humanity and his subjection to time and space (that is, to the Syrian life of his period) involved his belief in many things, true and false, that in no way distinguish him from other Syrians of that time. But such common beliefs do not constitute specific Christianity any more than wearing a beard, working in a carpenter's shop, or believing that the earth is flat and that the stars could drop on it from heaven like hailstones. Christianity interests practical statesmen now because of the doctrines that distinguished Christ from the Jews and the Barabbasques generally, including ourselves.

WHY JESUS MORE THAN ANOTHER?

I do not imply, however, that these doctrines were peculiar to Christ. A doctrine peculiar to one man would be only a craze, unless its comprehension depended on a development of human faculty so rare that only one exceptionally gifted man possessed it. But even in this case it would be useless, because incapable of spreading. Christianity is a step in moral evolution which is independent of any individual preacher. If Jesus had never existed (and that he ever existed in any other sense than that in which Shakespear's Hamlet existed has been vigorously questioned) Tolstoy would have thought and taught and quarrelled with the Greek Church all the same. Their creed has been fragmentarily practised to a considerable extent in spite of the fact that the laws of all countries treat it, in effect, as criminal. Many of its advocates have been militant atheists. But for some reason the imagination of white mankind has picked out Jesus of Nazareth as THE Christ, and attributed all the Christian doctrines to him; and as it is the doctrine and not the man that matters, and, as, besides, one symbol is as good as another provided everyone attaches the same meaning to it, I raise, for the moment, no question as to how far the gospels are original, and how far they consist of Greek and Chinese interpolations. The record that Jesus said certain things is not invalidated by a demonstration that Confucius said them before him. Those who claim a literal divine paternity for him cannot be silenced by the discovery that the same claim was made for Alexander and Augustus. And I am not just now concerned with the credibility of the gospels as records of fact; for I am not acting as a detective, but turning our modern lights on to certain ideas and doctrines in them which disentangle themselves from the rest because they are flatly contrary to common practice, common sense, and common belief, and yet have, in the teeth of dogged incredulity and recalcitrance, produced an irresistible impression that Christ, though rejected by his posterity as an unpractical dreamer, and executed by his contemporaries as a dangerous anarchist and blasphemous madman, was greater than his judges.

WAS JESUS A COWARD?

I know quite well that this impression of superiority is not produced on everyone, even of those who profess extreme susceptibility to it. Setting aside the huge mass of inculcated Christ-worship which has no real significance because it has no intelligence, there is, among people who are really free to think for themselves on the subject, a great deal of hearty dislike of Jesus and of contempt for his failure to save himself and overcome his enemies by personal bravery and cunning as Mahomet did. I have heard this feeling expressed far more impatiently by persons brought up in England as Christians than by Mahometans, who are, like their prophet, very civil to Jesus, and allow him a place in their esteem and veneration at least as high as we accord to John the Baptist. But this British bulldog contempt is founded on a complete misconception of his reasons for submitting voluntarily to an ordeal of torment and death. The modern Secularist is often so determined to regard Jesus as a man like himself and nothing more, that he slips unconsciously into the error of assuming that Jesus shared that view. But it is quite clear from the New Testament writers (the chief authorities for believing that Jesus ever existed) that Jesus at the time of his death believed himself to be the Christ, a divine personage. It is therefore absurd to criticize his conduct before Pilate as if he were Colonel Roosevelt or Admiral von Tirpitz or even Mahomet. Whether you accept his belief in his divinity as fully as Simon Peter did, or reject it as a delusion which led him to submit to torture and sacrifice his life without resistance in the conviction that he would presently rise again in glory, you are equally bound to admit that, far from behaving like a coward or a sheep, he showed considerable physical fortitude in going through a cruel ordeal against which he could have defended himself as effectually as he cleared the moneychangers out of the temple. "Gentle Jesus, meek and mild" is a snivelling modern invention, with no warrant in the gospels. St. Matthew would as soon have thought of applying such adjectives to Judas Maccabeus as to Jesus; and even St. Luke, who makes Jesus polite and gracious, does not make him meek. The picture of him as an English curate of the farcical comedy type, too meek to fight a policeman, and everybody's butt, may be useful in the nursery to soften children; but that such a figure could ever have become a centre of the world's attention is too absurd for discussion; grown men and women may speak kindly of a harmless creature who utters amiable sentiments and is a helpless nincompoop when he is called on to defend them; but they will not follow him, nor do what he tells them, because they do not wish to share his defeat and disgrace.

WAS JESUS A MARTYR?

It is important therefore that we should clear our minds of the notion that Jesus died, as some are in the habit of declaring, for his social and political opinions. There have been many martyrs to those opinions; but he was not one of them, nor, as his words show, did he see any more sense in martyrdom than Galileo did. He was executed by the Jews for the blasphemy of claiming to be a God; and Pilate, to whom this was a mere piece of superstitious nonsense, let them execute him as the cheapest way of keeping them quiet, on the formal plea that he had committed treason against Rome by saying that he was the King of the Jews. He was not falsely accused, nor denied full opportunities of defending himself. The proceedings were quite straightforward and regular; and Pilate, to whom the appeal lay, favored him and despised his judges, and was evidently willing enough to be conciliated. But instead of denying the charge, Jesus repeated the offence. He knew what he was doing: he had alienated numbers of his own disciples and been stoned in the streets for doing it before. He was not lying: he believed literally what he said. The horror of the High Priest was perfectly natural: he was a Primate confronted with a heterodox street preacher uttering what seemed to him an appalling and impudent blasphemy. The fact that the blasphemy was to Jesus a simple statement of fact, and that it has since been accepted as such by all western nations, does not invalidate the proceedings, nor give us the right to regard Annas and Caiaphas as worse men than the Archbishop of Canterbury and the Head Master of Eton. If Jesus had been indicted in a modern court, he would have been examined by two doctors; found to be obsessed by a delusion; declared incapable of pleading; and sent to an asylum: that is the whole difference. But please note that when a man is charged before a modern tribunal (to take a case that happened the other day) of having asserted and maintained that he was an officer returned from the front to receive the Victoria Cross at the hands of the King, although he was in fact a mechanic, nobody thinks of treating him as afflicted with a delusion. He is punished for false pretences, because his assertion is credible and therefore misleading. Just so, the claim to divinity made by Jesus was to the High Priest, who looked forward to the coming of a Messiah, one that might conceivably have been true, and might therefore have misled the people in a very dangerous way. That was why he treated Jesus as an imposter and a blasphemer where we should have treated him as a madman.

THE GOSPELS WITHOUT PREJUDICE.

All this will become clear if we read the gospels without prejudice. When I was young it was impossible to read them without fantastic confusion of thought. The confusion was so utterly confounded that it was called the proper spirit to read the Bible in. Jesus was a baby; and he was older than creation. He was a man who could be persecuted, stoned, scourged, and killed; and he was a god, immortal and all-powerful, able to raise the dead and call millions of angels to his aid. It was a sin to doubt either view of him: that is, it was a sin to reason about him; and the end was that you did not reason about him, and read about him only when you were compelled. When you heard the gospel stories read in church, or learnt them from painters and poets, you came out with an impression of their contents that would have astonished a Chinaman who had read the story without prepossession. Even sceptics who were specially on their guard, put the Bible in the dock, and read the gospels with the object of detecting discrepancies in the four narratives to show that the writers were as subject to error as the writers of yesterday's newspaper.

All this has changed greatly within two generations. Today the Bible is so little read that the language of the Authorized Version is rapidly becoming obsolete; so that even in the United States, where the old tradition of the verbal infallibility of "the book of books" lingers more strongly than anywhere else except perhaps in Ulster, retranslations into modern English have been introduced perforce to save its bare intelligibility. It is quite easy today to find cultivated persons who have never read the New Testament, and on whom therefore it is possible to try the experiment of asking them to read the gospels and state what they have gathered as to the history and views and character of Christ.

THE GOSPELS NOW UNINTELLIGIBLE TO NOVICES.

But it will not do to read the gospels with a mind furnished only for the reception of, say, a biography of Goethe. You will not make sense of them, nor even be able without impatient weariness to persevere in the task of going steadily through them, unless you know something of the history of the human imagination as applied to religion. Not long ago I asked a writer of distinguished intellectual competence whether he had made a study of the gospels since his childhood. His reply was that he had lately tried, but "found it all such nonsense that I could not stick it." As I do not want to send anyone to the gospels with this result, I had better here give a brief exposition of how much of the history of religion is needed to make the gospels and the conduct and ultimate fate of Jesus intelligible and interesting.

WORLDLINESS OF THE MAJORITY.

The first common mistake to get rid of is that mankind consists of a great mass of religious people and a few eccentric atheists. It consists of a huge mass of worldly people, and a small percentage of persons deeply interested in religion and concerned about their own souls and other peoples'; and this section consists mostly of those who are passionately affirming the established religion and those who are passionately attacking it, the genuine philosophers being very few. Thus you never have a nation of millions of Wesleys and one Tom Paine. You have a million Mr. Worldly Wisemans, one Wesley, with his small congregation, and one Tom Paine, with his smaller congregation. The passionately religious are a people apart; and if they were not hopelessly outnumbered by the worldly, they would turn the world upside down, as St. Paul was reproached, quite justly, for wanting to do. Few people can number among their personal acquaintances a single atheist or a single Plymouth Brother. Unless a religious turn in ourselves has led us to seek the little Societies to which these rare birds belong, we pass our lives among people who, whatever creeds they may repeat, and in whatever temples they may avouch their respectability and wear their Sunday clothes, have robust consciences, and hunger and thirst, not for righteousness, but for rich feeding and comfort and social position and attractive mates and ease and pleasure and respect and consideration: in short, for love and money. To these people one morality is as good as another provided they are used to it and can put up with its restrictions without unhappiness; and in the maintenance of this morality they will fight and punish and coerce without scruple. They may not be the salt of the earth, these Philistines; but they are the substance of civilization; and they save society from ruin by criminals and conquerors as well as by Savonarolas and Knipperdollings. And as they know, very sensibly, that a little religion is good for children and serves morality, keeping the poor in good humor or in awe by promising rewards in heaven or threatening torments in hell, they encourage the religious people up to a certain point: for instance, if Savonarola only tells the ladies of Florence that they ought to tear off their jewels and finery and sacrifice them to God, they offer him a cardinal's hat, and praise him as a saint; but if he induces them to actually do it, they burn him as a public nuisance.

RELIGION OF THE MINORITY. SALVATIONISM.

The religion of the tolerated religious minority has always been essentially the same religion: that is why its changes of name and form have made so little difference. That is why, also, a nation so civilized as the English can convert negroes to their faith with great ease, but cannot convert Mahometans or Jews. The negro finds in civilized Salvationism an unspeakably more comforting version of his crude creed; but neither Saracen nor Jew sees any advantage in it over his own version. The Crusader was surprised to find the Saracen quite as religious and moral as himself, and rather more than less civilized. The Latin Christian has nothing to offer the Greek Christian that Greek Christianity has not already provided. They are all, at root, Salvationists.

Let us trace this religion of Salvation from its beginnings. So many things that man does not himself contrive or desire are always happening: death, plagues, tempests, blights, floods, sunrise and sunset, growths and harvests and decay, and Kant's two wonders of the starry heavens above us and the moral law within us, that we conclude that somebody must be doing it all, or that somebody is doing the good and somebody else doing the evil, or that armies of invisible persons, benefit-cut and malevolent, are doing it; hence you postulate gods and devils, angels and demons. You propitiate these powers with presents, called sacrifices, and flatteries, called praises. Then the Kantian moral law within you makes you conceive your god as a judge; and straightway you try to corrupt him, also with presents and flatteries. This seems shocking to us; but our objection to it is quite a recent development: no longer ago than Shakespear's time it was thought quite natural that litigants should give presents to human judges; and the buying off of divine wrath by actual money payments to priests, or, in the reformed churches which discountenance this, by subscriptions to charities and church building and the like, is still in full swing. Its practical disadvantage is that though it makes matters very easy for the rich, it cuts off the poor from all hope of divine favor. And this quickens the moral criticism of the poor to such an extent, that they soon find the moral law within them revolting against the idea of buying off the deity with gold and gifts, though they are still quite ready to buy him off with the paper money of praise and professions of repentance. Accordingly, you will find that though a religion may last unchanged for many centuries in primitive communities where the conditions of life leave no room for poverty and riches, and the process of propitiating the supernatural powers is as well within the means of the least of the members as within those of the headman, yet when commercial civilization arrives, and capitalism divides the people into a few rich and a great many so poor that they can barely live, a movement for religious reform will arise among the poor, and will be essentially a movement for cheap or entirely gratuitous salvation. To understand what the poor mean by propitiation, we must examine for a moment what they mean by justice.

THE DIFFERENCE BETWEEN ATONEMENT AND PUNISHMENT

The primitive idea of justice is partly legalized revenge and partly expiation by sacrifice. It works out from both sides in the notion that two blacks make a white, and that when a wrong has been done, it should be paid for by an equivalent suffering. It seems to the Philistine majority a matter of course that this compensating suffering should be inflicted on the wrongdoer for the sake of its deterrent effect on other would-be wrongdoers; but a moment's reflection will show that this utilitarian application corrupts the whole transaction. For example, the shedding of innocent blood cannot be balanced by the shedding of guilty blood. Sacrificing a criminal to propitiate God for the murder of one of his righteous servants is like sacrificing a mangy sheep or an ox with the rinderpest: it calls down divine wrath instead of appeasing it. In doing it we offer God as a sacrifice the gratification of our own revenge and the protection of our own lives without cost to ourselves; and cost to ourselves is the essence of sacrifice and expiation. However much the Philistines have succeeded in confusing these things in practice, they are to the Salvationist sense distinct and even contrary. The Baronet's cousin in Dickens's novel, who, perplexed by the failure of the police to discover the murderer of the baronet's solicitor, said "Far better hang wrong fellow than no fellow," was not only expressing a very common sentiment, but trembling on the brink of the rarer Salvationist opinion that it is much better to hang the wrong fellow: that, in fact, the wrong fellow is the right fellow to hang.

The point is a cardinal one, because until we grasp it not only does historical Christianity remain unintelligible to us, but those who do not care a rap about historical Christianity may be led into the mistake of supposing that if we discard revenge, and treat murderers exactly as God treated Cain: that is, exempt them from punishment by putting a brand on them as unworthy to be sacrificed, and let them face the world as best they can with that brand on them, we should get rid both of punishment and sacrifice. It would not at all follow: on the contrary, the feeling that there must be an expiation of the murder might quite possibly lead to our putting some innocent person--the more innocent the better--to a cruel death to balance the account with divine justice.

SALVATION AT FIRST A CLASS PRIVILEGE; AND THE REMEDY

Thus, even when the poor decide that the method of purchasing salvation by offering rams and goats or bringing gold to the altar must be wrong because they cannot afford it, we still do not feel "saved" without a sacrifice and a victim. In vain do we try to substitute mystical rites that cost nothing, such as circumcision, or, as a substitute for that, baptism. Our sense of justice still demands an expiation, a sacrifice, a sufferer for our sins. And this leaves the poor man still in his old difficulty; for if it was impossible for him to procure rams and goats and shekels, how much more impossible is it for him to find a neighbor who will voluntarily suffer for his sins: one who will say cheerfully "You have committed a murder. Well, never mind: I am willing to be hanged for it in your stead?"

Our imagination must come to our rescue. Why not, instead of driving ourselves to despair by insisting on a separate atonement by a separate redeemer for every sin, have one great atonement and one great redeemer to compound for the sins of the world once for all? Nothing easier, nothing cheaper. The yoke is easy, the burden light. All you have to do when the redeemer is once found (or invented by the imagination) is to believe in the efficacy of the transaction, and you are saved. The rams and goats cease to bleed; the altars which ask for expensive gifts and continually renewed sacrifices are torn down; and the Church of the single redeemer and the single atonement rises on the ruins of the old temples, and becomes a single Church of the Christ.

RETROSPECTIVE ATONEMENT, AND THE EXPECTATION OF THE REDEEMER

But this does not happen at once. Between the old costly religion of the rich and the new gratuitous religion of the poor there comes an interregnum in which the redeemer, though conceived by the human imagination, is not yet found. He is awaited and expected under the names of the Christ, the Messiah, Baldur the Beautiful, or what not; but he has not yet come. Yet the sinners are not therefore in despair. It is true that they cannot say, as we say, "The Christ has come, and has redeemed us;" but they can say "The Christ will come, and will redeem us," which, as the atonement is conceived as retrospective, is equally consoling. There are periods when nations are seething with this expectation and crying aloud with prophecy of the Redeemer through their poets. To feel that atmosphere we have only to take up the Bible and read Isaiah at one end of such a period and Luke and John at the other.

COMPLETION OF THE SCHEME BY LUTHER AND CALVIN

We now see our religion as a quaint but quite intelligible evolution from crude attempts to propitiate the destructive forces of Nature among savages to a subtle theology with a costly ritual of sacrifice possible only to the rich as a luxury, and finally to the religion of Luther and Calvin. And it must be said for the earlier forms that they involved very real sacrifices. The sacrifice was not always vicarious, and is not yet universally so. In India men pay with their own skins, torturing themselves hideously to attain holiness. In the west, saints amazed the world with their austerities and self-scourgings and confessions and vigils. But Luther delivered us from all that. His reformation was a triumph of imagination and a triumph of cheapness. It brought you complete salvation and asked you for nothing but faith. Luther did not know what he was doing in the scientific sociological way in which we know it; but his instinct served him better than knowledge could have done; for it was instinct rather than theological casuistry that made him hold so resolutely to Justification by Faith as the trump card by which he should beat the Pope, or, as he would have put it, the sign in which he should conquer. He may be said to have abolished the charge for admission to heaven. Paul had advocated this; but Luther and Calvin did it.

JOHN BARLEYCORN

There is yet another page in the history of religion which must be conned and digested before the career of Jesus can be fully understood. people who can read long books will find it in Frazer's Golden Bough. Simpler folk will find it in the peasant's song of John Barleycorn, now made accessible to our drawingroom amateurs in the admirable collections of Somersetshire Folk Songs by Mr. Cecil Sharp. From Frazer's magnum opus you will learn how the same primitive logic which makes the Englishman believe today that by eating a beefsteak he can acquire the strength and courage of the bull, and to hold that belief in the face of the most ignominious defeats by vegetarian wrestlers and racers and bicyclists, led the first men who conceived God as capable of incarnation to believe that they could acquire a spark of his divinity by eating his flesh and drinking his blood. And from the song of John Barleycorn you may learn how the miracle of the seed, the growth, and the harvest, still the most wonderful of all the miracles and as inexplicable as ever, taught the primitive husbandman, and, as we must now affirm, taught him quite rightly, that God is in the seed, and that God is immortal. And thus it became the test of Godhead that nothing that you could do to it could kill it, and that when you buried it, it would rise again in renewed life and beauty and give mankind eternal life on condition that it was eaten and drunk, and again slain and buried, to rise again for ever and ever. You may, and indeed must, use John Barleycorn "right barbarouslee," cutting him "off at knee" with your scythes, scourging him with your flails, burying him in the earth; and he will not resist you nor reproach you, but will rise again in golden beauty amidst a great burst of sunshine and bird music, and save you and renew your life. And from the interweaving of these two traditions with the craving for the Redeemer, you at last get the conviction that when the Redeemer comes he will be immortal; he will give us his body to eat and his blood to drink; and he will prove his divinity by suffering a barbarous death without resistance or reproach, and rise from the dead and return to the earth in glory as the giver of life eternal.

LOOKING FOR THE END OF THE WORLD

Yet another persistent belief has beset the imagination of the religious ever since religion spread among the poor, or, rather, ever since commercial civilization produced a hopelessly poor class cut off from enjoyment in this world. That belief is that the end of this world is at hand, and that it will presently pass away and be replaced by a kingdom of happiness, justice, and bliss in which the rich and the oppressors and the unjust shall have no share. We are all familiar with this expectation: many of us cherish some pious relative who sees in every great calamity a sign of the approaching end. Warning pamphlets are in constant circulation: advertisements are put in the papers and paid for by those who are convinced, and who are horrified at the indifference of the irreligious to the approaching doom. And revivalist preachers, now as in the days of John the Baptist, seldom fail to warn their flocks to watch and pray, as the great day will steal upon them like a thief in the night, and cannot be long deferred in a world so wicked. This belief also associates itself with Barleycorn's second coming; so that the two events become identified at last.

There is the other and more artificial side of this belief, on which it is an inculcated dread. The ruler who appeals to the prospect of heaven to console the poor and keep them from insurrection also curbs the vicious by threatening them with hell. In the Koran we find Mahomet driven more and more to this expedient of government; and experience confirms his evident belief that it is impossible to govern without it in certain phases of civilization. We shall see later on that it gives a powerful attraction to the belief in a Redeemer, since it adds to remorse of conscience, which hardened men bear very lightly, a definite dread of hideous and eternal torture.

THE HONOR OF DIVINE PARENTAGE

One more tradition must be noted. The consummation of praise for a king is to declare that he is the son of no earthly father, but of a god. His mother goes into the temple of Apollo, and Apollo comes to her in the shape of a serpent, or the like. The Roman emperors, following the example of Augustus, claimed the title of God. Illogically, such divine kings insist a good deal on their royal human ancestors. Alexander, claiming to be the son of Apollo, is equally determined to be the son of Philip. As the gospels stand, St. Matthew and St. Luke give genealogies (the two are different) establishing the descent of Jesus through Joseph from the royal house of David, and yet declare that not Joseph but the Holy Ghost was the father of Jesus. It is therefore now held that the story of the Holy Ghost is a later interpolation borrowed from the Greek and Roman imperial tradition. But experience shows that simultaneous faith in the descent from David and the conception by the Holy Ghost is possible. Such double beliefs are entertained by the human mind without uneasiness or consciousness of the contradiction involved. Many instances might be given: a familiar one to my generation being that of the Tichborne claimant, whose attempt to pass himself off as a baronet was supported by an association of laborers on the ground that the Tichborne family, in resisting it, were trying to do a laborer out of his rights. It is quite possible that Matthew and Luke may have been unconscious of the contradiction: indeed the interpolation theory does not remove the difficulty, as the interpolators themselves must have been unconscious of it. A better ground for suspecting interpolation is that St. Paul knew nothing of the divine birth, and taught that Jesus came into the world at his birth as the son of Joseph, but rose from the dead after three days as the son of God. Here again, few notice the discrepancy: the three views are accepted simultaneously without intellectual discomfort. We can provisionally entertain half a dozen contradictory versions of an event if we feel either that it does not greatly matter, or that there is a category attainable in which the contradictions are reconciled.

But that is not the present point. All that need be noted here is that the legend of divine birth was sure to be attached sooner or later to very eminent persons in Roman imperial times, and that modern theologians, far from discrediting it, have very logically affirmed the miraculous conception not only of Jesus but of his mother.

With no more scholarly equipment than a knowledge of these habits of the human imagination, anyone may now read the four gospels without bewilderment, and without the contemptuous incredulity which spoils the temper of many modern atheists, or the senseless credulity which sometimes makes pious people force us to shove them aside in emergencies as impracticable lunatics when they ask us to meet violence and injustice with dumb submission in the belief that the strange demeanor of Jesus before Pilate was meant as an example of normal human conduct. Let us admit that without the proper clues the gospels are, to a modern educated person, nonsensical and incredible, whilst the apostles are unreadable. But with the clues, they are fairly plain sailing. Jesus becomes an intelligible and consistent person. His reasons for going "like a lamb to the slaughter" instead of saving himself as Mahomet did, become quite clear. The narrative becomes as credible as any other historical narrative of its period.

MATTHEW.
THE ANNUNCIATION: THE MASSACRE:
THE FLIGHT

Let us begin with the gospel of Matthew, bearing in mind that it does not profess to be the evidence of an eyewitness. It is a chronicle, founded, like other chronicles, on such evidence and records as the chronicler could get hold of. The only one of the evangelists who professes to give first-hand evidence as an eyewitness naturally takes care to say so; and the fact that Matthew makes no such pretension, and writes throughout as a chronicler, makes it clear that he is telling the story of Jesus as Holinshed told the story of Macbeth, except that, for a reason to be given later on, he must have collected his material and completed his book within the lifetime of persons contemporary with Jesus. Allowance must also be made for the fact that the gospel is written in the Greek language, whilst the first-hand traditions and the actual utterances of Jesus must have been in Aramaic, the dialect of Palestine. These distinctions were important, as you will find if you read Holinshed or Froissart and then read Benvenuto Cellini. You do not blame Holinshed or Froissart for believing and repeating the things they had read or been told, though you cannot always believe these things yourself. But when Cellini tells you that he saw this or did that, and you find it impossible to believe him, you lose patience with him, and are disposed to doubt everything in his autobiography. Do not forget, then, that Matthew is Holinshed and not Benvenuto. The very first pages of his narrative will put your attitude to the test.

Matthew tells us that the mother of Jesus was betrothed to a man of royal pedigree named Joseph, who was rich enough to live in a house in Bethlehem to which kings could bring gifts of gold without provoking any comment. An angel announces to Joseph that Jesus is the son of the Holy Ghost, and that he must not accuse her of infidelity because of her bearing a son of which he is not the father; but this episode disappears from the subsequent narrative: there is no record of its having been told to Jesus, nor any indication of his having any knowledge of it. The narrative, in fact, proceeds in all respects as if the annunciation formed no part of it.

Herod the Tetrarch, believing that a child has been born who will destroy him, orders all the male children to be slaughtered; and Jesus escapes by the flight of his parents into Egypt, whence they return to Nazareth when the danger is over. Here it is necessary to anticipate a little by saying that none of the other evangelists accept this story, as none of them except John, who throws over Matthew altogether, shares his craze for treating history and biography as mere records of the fulfillment of ancient Jewish prophecies. This craze no doubt led him to seek for some legend bearing out Hosea's "Out of Egypt have I called my son," and Jeremiah's Rachel weeping for her children: in fact, he says so. Nothing that interests us nowadays turns on the credibility of the massacre of the innocents and the flight into Egypt. We may forget them, and proceed to the important part of the narrative, which skips at once to the manhood of Jesus.

JOHN THE BAPTIST

At this moment, a Salvationist prophet named John is stirring the people very strongly. John has declared that the rite of circumcision is insufficient as a dedication of the individual to God, and has substituted the rite of baptism. To us, who are accustomed to baptism as a matter of course, and to whom circumcision is a rather ridiculous foreign practice of no consequence, the sensational effect of such a heresy as this on the Jews is not apparent: it seems to us as natural that John should have baptized people as that the rector of our village should do so. But, as St. Paul found to his cost later on, the discarding of circumcision for baptism was to the Jews as startling a heresy as the discarding of transubstantiation in the Mass was to the Catholics of the XVI century.

JESUS JOINS THE BAPTISTS

Jesus entered as a man of thirty (Luke says) into the religious life of his time by going to John the Baptist and demanding baptism from him, much as certain well-to-do young gentlemen forty years ago "joined the Socialists." As far as established Jewry was concerned, he burnt his boats by this action, and cut himself off from the routine of wealth, respectability, and orthodoxy. He then began preaching John's gospel, which, apart from the heresy of baptism, the value of which lay in its bringing the Gentiles (that is, the uncircumcised) within the pale of salvation, was a call to the people to repent of their sins, as the kingdom of heaven was at hand. Luke adds that he also preached the communism of charity; told the surveyors of taxes not to over-assess the taxpayers; and advised soldiers to be content with their wages and not to be violent or lay false accusations. There is no record of John going beyond this.

THE SAVAGE JOHN AND THE CIVILIZED JESUS

Jesus went beyond it very rapidly, according to Matthew. Though, like John, he became an itinerant preacher, he departed widely from John's manner of life. John went into the wilderness, not into the synagogues; and his baptismal font was the river Jordan. He was an ascetic, clothed in skins and living on locusts and wild honey, practising a savage austerity. He courted martyrdom, and met it at the hands of Herod. Jesus saw no merit either in asceticism or martyrdom. In contrast to John he was essentially a highly-civilized, cultivated person. According to Luke, he pointed out the contrast himself, chaffing the Jews for complaining that John must be possessed by the devil because he was a teetotaller and vegetarian, whilst, because Jesus was neither one nor the other, they reviled him as a gluttonous man and a winebibber, the friend of the officials and their mistresses. He told straitlaced disciples that they would have trouble enough from other people without making any for themselves, and that they should avoid martyrdom and enjoy themselves whilst they had the chance. "When they persecute you in this city," he says, "flee into the next." He preaches in the synagogues and in the open air indifferently, just as they come. He repeatedly says, "I desire mercy and not sacrifice," meaning evidently to clear himself of the inveterate superstition that suffering is gratifying to God. "Be not, as the Pharisees, of a sad countenance," he says. He is convivial, feasting with Roman officials and sinners. He is careless of his person, and is remonstrated with for not washing his hands before sitting down to table. The followers of John the Baptist, who fast, and who expect to find the Christians greater ascetics than themselves, are disappointed at finding that Jesus and his twelve friends do not fast; and Jesus tells them that they should rejoice in him instead of being melancholy. He is jocular and tells them they will all have as much fasting as they want soon enough, whether they like it or not. He is not afraid of disease, and dines with a leper. A woman, apparently to protect him against infection, pours a costly unguent on his head, and is rebuked because what it cost might have been given to the poor. He poohpoohs that lowspirited view, and says, as he said when he was reproached for not fasting, that the poor are always there to be helped, but that he is not there to be anointed always, implying that you should never lose a chance of being happy when there is so much misery in the world. He breaks the Sabbath; is impatient of conventionality when it is uncomfortable or obstructive; and outrages the feelings of the Jews by breaches of it. He is apt to accuse people who feel that way of hypocrisy. Like the late Samuel Butler, he regards disease as a department of sin, and on curing a lame man, says "Thy sins are forgiven" instead of "Arise and walk," subsequently maintaining, when the Scribes reproach him for assuming power to forgive sin as well as to cure disease, that the two come to the same thing. He has no modest affectations, and claims to be greater than Solomon or Jonah. When reproached, as Bunyan was, for resorting to the art of fiction when teaching in parables, he justifies himself on the ground that art is the only way in which the people can be taught. He is, in short, what we should call an artist and a Bohemian in his manner of life.

JESUS NOT A PROSLETYST

A point of considerable practical importance today is that be expressly repudiates the idea that forms of religion, once rooted, can be weeded out and replanted with the flowers of a foreign faith. "If you try to root up the tares you will root up the wheat as well." Our proselytizing missionary enterprises are thus flatly contrary to his advice; and their results appear to bear him out in his view that if you convert a man brought up in another creed, you inevitably demoralize him. He acts on this view himself, and does not convert his disciples from Judaism to Christianity. To this day a Christian would be in religion a Jew initiated by baptism instead of circumcision, and accepting Jesus as the Messiah, and his teachings as of higher authority than those of Moses, but for the action of the Jewish priests, who, to save Jewry from being submerged in the rising flood of Christianity after the capture of Jerusalem and the destruction of the Temple, set up what was practically a new religious order, with new Scriptures and elaborate new observances, and to their list of the accursed added one Jeschu, a bastard magician, whose comic rogueries brought him to a bad end like Punch or Til Eulenspiegel: an invention which cost them dear when the Christians got the upper hand of them politically. The Jew as Jesus, himself a Jew, knew him, never dreamt of such things, and could follow Jesus without ceasing to be a Jew.

THE TEACHINGS OF JESUS.

So much for his personal life and temperament. His public career as a popular preacher carries him equally far beyond John the Baptist. He lays no stress on baptism or vows, and preaches conduct incessantly. He advocates communism, the widening of the private family with its cramping ties into the great family of mankind under the fatherhood of God, the abandonment of revenge and punishment, the counteracting of evil by good instead of by a hostile evil, and an organic conception of society in which you are not an independent individual but a member of society, your neighbor being another member, and each of you members one of another, as two fingers on a hand, the obvious conclusion being that unless you love your neighbor as yourself and he reciprocates you will both be the worse for it. He conveys all this with extraordinary charm, and entertains his hearers with fables (parables) to illustrate them. He has no synagogue or regular congregation, but travels from place to place with twelve men whom he has called from their work as he passed, and who have abandoned it to follow him.

THE MIRACLES

He has certain abnormal powers by which he can perform miracles. He is ashamed of these powers, but, being extremely compassionate, cannot refuse to exercise them when afflicted people beg him to cure them, when multitudes of people are hungry, and when his disciples are terrified by storms on the lakes. He asks for no reward, but begs the people not to mention these powers of his. There are two obvious reasons for his dislike of being known as a worker of miracles. One is the natural objection of all men who possess such powers, but have far more important business in the world than to exhibit them, to be regarded primarily as charlatans, besides being pestered to give exhibitions to satisfy curiosity. The other is that his view of the effect of miracles upon his mission is exactly that taken later on by Rousseau. He perceives that they will discredit him and divert attention from his doctrine by raising an entirely irrelevant issue between his disciples and his opponents.

Possibly my readers may not have studied Rousseau's Letters Written From The Mountain, which may be regarded as the classic work on miracles as credentials of divine mission. Rousseau shows, as Jesus foresaw, that the miracles are the main obstacle to the acceptance of Christianity, because their incredibility (if they were not incredible they would not be miracles) makes people sceptical as to the whole narrative, credible enough in the main, in which they occur, and suspicious of the doctrine with which they are thus associated. "Get rid of the miracles," said

Rousseau, "and the whole world will fall at the feet of Jesus Christ." He points out that miracles offered as evidence of divinity, and failing to convince, make divinity ridiculous. He says, in effect, there is nothing in making a lame man walk: thousands of lame men have been cured and have walked without any miracle. Bring me a man with only one leg and make another grow instantaneously on him before my eyes; and I will be really impressed; but mere cures of ailments that have often been cured before are quite useless as evidence of anything else than desire to help and power to cure.

Jesus, according to Matthew, agreed so entirely with Rousseau, and felt the danger so strongly, that when people who were not ill or in trouble came to him and asked him to exercise his powers as a sign of his mission, he was irritated beyond measure, and refused with an indignation which they, not seeing Rousseau's point, must have thought very unreasonable. To be called "an evil and adulterous generation" merely for asking a miracle worker to give an exhibition of his powers, is rather a startling experience. Mahomet, by the way, also lost his temper when people asked him to perform miracles. But Mahomet expressly disclaimed any unusual powers; whereas it is clear from Matthew's story that Jesus (unfortunately for himself, as he thought) had some powers of healing. It is also obvious that the exercise of such powers would give rise to wild tales of magical feats which would expose their hero to condemnation as an impostor among people whose good opinion was of great consequence to the movement started by his mission.

But the deepest annoyance arising from the miracles would be the irrelevance of the issue raised by them. Jesus's teaching has nothing to do with miracles. If his mission had been simply to demonstrate a new method of restoring lost eyesight, the miracle of curing the blind would have been entirely relevant. But to say "You should love your enemies; and to convince you of this I will now proceed to cure this gentleman of cataract" would have been, to a man of Jesus's intelligence, the proposition of an idiot. If it could be proved today that not one of the miracles of Jesus actually occurred, that proof would not invalidate a single one of his didactic utterances; and conversely, if it could be proved that not only did the miracles actually occur, but that he had wrought a thousand other miracles a thousand times more wonderful, not a jot of weight would be added to his doctrine. And yet the intellectual energy of sceptics and divines has been wasted for generations in arguing about the miracles on the assumption that Christianity is at stake in the controversy as to whether the stories of Matthew are false or true. According to Matthew himself, Jesus must have known this only too well; for wherever he went he was assailed with a clamor for miracles, though his doctrine created bewilderment.

So much for the miracles! Matthew tells us further, that Jesus declared that his doctrines would be attacked by Church and State, and that the common multitude were the salt of the earth and the light of the world. His disciples, in their relations with the political and ecclesiastical organizations, would be as sheep among wolves.

MATTHEW IMPUTES DIGNITY TO JESUS.

Matthew, like most biographers, strives to identify the opinions and prejudices of his hero with his own. Although he describes Jesus as tolerant even to carelessness, he draws the line at the Gentile, and represents Jesus as a bigoted Jew who regards his mission as addressed exclusively to "the lost sheep of the house of Israel." When a woman of Canaan begged Jesus to cure her daughter, he first refused to speak to her, and then told her brutally that "It is not meet to take the children's bread and cast it to the dogs." But when the woman said, "Truth, Lord; yet the dogs eat of the crumbs which fall from their master's table," she melted the Jew out of him and made Christ a Christian. To the woman whom he had just called a dog he said, "O woman, great is thy faith: be it unto thee even as thou wilt." This is somehow one of the most touching stories in the gospel; perhaps because the woman rebukes the prophet by a touch of his own finest quality. It is certainly out of character; but as the sins of good men are always out of character, it is not safe to reject the story as invented in the interest of Matthew's determination that Jesus shall have nothing to do with the Gentiles. At all events, there the story is; and it is by no means the only instance in which Matthew reports Jesus, in spite of the charm of his preaching, as extremely uncivil in private intercourse.

THE GREAT CHANGE.

So far the history is that of a man sane and interesting apart from his special gifts as orator, healer, and prophet. But a startling change occurs. One day, after the disciples have discouraged him for a long time by their misunderstandings of his mission, and their speculations as to whether he is one of the old prophets come again, and if so, which, his disciple Peter suddenly solves the problem by exclaiming, "Thou are the Christ, the son of the living God." At this Jesus is extraordinarily pleased and excited. He declares that Peter has had a revelation straight from God. He makes a pun on Peter's name, and declares him the founder of his Church. And he accepts his destiny as a god by announcing that he will be killed when he goes to Jerusalem; for if he is really the Christ, it is a necessary part of his legendary destiny that he shall be slain. Peter, not understanding this, rebukes him for what seems mere craven melancholy; and Jesus turns fiercely on him and cries, "Get thee behind me, Satan."

Jesus now becomes obsessed with a conviction of his divinity, and talks about it continually to his disciples, though he forbids them to mention it to others. They begin to dispute among themselves as to the position they shall occupy in heaven when his kingdom is established. He rebukes them strenuously for this, and repeats his teaching that greatness means service and not domination; but he himself, always instinctively somewhat haughty, now becomes arrogant, dictatorial, and even abusive, never replying to his critics without an insulting epithet, and even cursing a fig-tree which disappoints him when he goes to it for fruit. He assumes all the traditions of the folk-lore gods, and announces that, like John Barleycorn, he will be barbarously slain and buried, but will rise from the earth and return to life. He attaches to himself the immemorial tribal ceremony of eating the god, by blessing bread and wine and handing them to his disciples with the words "This is my body: this is my blood." He forgets his own teaching and threatens eternal fire and eternal punishment. He announces, in addition to his Barleycorn resurrection, that he will come to the world a second time in glory and establish his kingdom on earth. He fears that this may lead to the appearance of impostors claiming to be himself, and declares explicitly and repeatedly that no matter what wonders these impostors may perform, his own coming will be unmistakable, as the stars will fall from heaven, and trumpets be blown by angels. Further he declares that this will take place during the lifetime of persons then present,

JERUSALEM AND THE MYSTICAL SACRIFICE.

In this new frame of mind he at last enters Jerusalem amid great popular curiosity; drives the moneychangers and sacrifice sellers out of the temple in a riot; refuses to interest himself in the beauties and wonders of the temple building on the ground that presently not a stone of it shall be left on another; reviles the high priests and elders in intolerable terms; and is arrested by night in a garden to avoid a popular disturbance. He makes no resistance, being persuaded that it is part of his destiny as a god to be murdered and to rise again. One of his followers shows fight, and cuts off the ear of one of his captors. Jesus rebukes him, but does not attempt to heal the wound, though he declares that if he wished to resist he could easily summon twelve million angels to his aid. He is taken before the high priest and by him handed over to the Roman governor, who is puzzled by his silent refusal to defend himself in any way, or to contradict his accusers or their witnesses, Pilate having naturally no idea that the prisoner conceives himself as going through an inevitable process of torment, death, and burial as a prelude to resurrection. Before the high priest he has also been silent except that when the priest asks him is he the Christ, the Son of God, he replies that they shall all see the Son of Man sitting at the right hand of power, and coming on the clouds of heaven. He maintains this attitude with frightful fortitude whilst they scourge him, mock him, torment him, and finally crucify him between two thieves. His prolonged agony of thirst and pain on the cross at last breaks his spirit, and he dies with a cry of "My God: why hast Thou forsaken me?"

NOT THIS MAN BUT BARRABAS

Meanwhile he has been definitely rejected by the people as well as by the priests. Pilate, pitying him, and unable to make out exactly what he has done (the blasphemy that has horrified the high priest does not move the Roman) tries to get him off by reminding the people that they have, by custom, the right to have a prisoner released at that time, and suggests that he should release Jesus. But they insist on his releasing a prisoner named Barabbas instead, and on having Jesus crucified. Matthew gives no clue to the popularity of Barabbas, describing him simply as "a notable prisoner." The later gospels make it clear, very significantly, that his offence was sedition and insurrection; that he was an advocate of physical force; and that he had killed his man. The choice of Barabbas thus appears as a popular choice of the militant advocate of physical force as against the unresisting advocate of mercy.

THE RESURRECTION.

Matthew then tells how after three days an angel opened the family vault of one Joseph, a rich man of Arimathea, who had buried Jesus in it, whereupon Jesus rose and returned from Jerusalem to Galilee and resumed his preaching with his disciples, assuring them that he would now be with them to the end of the world. At that point the narrative abruptly stops. The story has no ending.

DATE OF MATTHEW'S NARRATIVE.

One effect of the promise of Jesus to come again in glory during the lifetime of some of his hearers is to date the gospel without the aid of any scholarship. It must have been written during the lifetime of Jesus's contemporaries: that is, whilst it was still possible for the promise of his Second Coming to be fulfilled. The death of the last person who had been alive when Jesus said "There be some of them that stand here that shall in no wise taste death till they see the Son of Man coming in his kingdom" destroyed the last possibility of the promised Second Coming, and bore out the incredulity of Pilate and the Jews. And as Matthew writes as one believing in that Second Coming, and in fact left his story unfinished to be ended by it, he must have produced his gospel within a lifetime of the crucifixion. Also, he must have believed that reading books would be one of the pleasures of the kingdom of heaven on earth.

CLASS TYPE OF MATTHEW'S JESUS

One more circumstance must be noted as gathered from Matthew. Though he begins his story in such a way as to suggest that Jesus belonged to the privileged classes, he mentions later on that when Jesus attempted to preach in his own country, and had no success there, the people said, "Is not this the carpenter's son?" But Jesus's manner throughout is that of an aristocrat, or at the very least the son of a rich bourgeois, and by no means a lowly-minded one at that. We must be careful therefore to conceive Joseph, not as a modern proletarian carpenter working for weekly wages, but as a master craftsman of royal descent. John the Baptist may have been a Keir Hardie; but the Jesus of Matthew is of the Ruskin-Morris class.

This haughty characterization is so marked that if we had no other documents concerning Jesus than the gospel of Matthew, we should not feel as we do about him. We should have been much less loth to say, "There is a man here who was sane until Peter hailed him as the Christ, and who then became a monomaniac." We should have pointed out that his delusion is a very common delusion among the insane, and that such insanity is quite consistent with the retention of the argumentative cunning and penetration which Jesus displayed in Jerusalem after his delusion had taken complete hold of him. We should feel horrified at the scourging and mocking and crucifixion just as we should if Ruskin had been treated in that way when he also went mad, instead of being cared for as an invalid. And we should have had no clear perception of any special significance in his way of calling the Son of God the Son of Man. We should have noticed that he was a Communist; that he regarded much of what we call law and order as machinery for robbing the poor under legal forms; that he thought domestic ties a snare for the soul; that he agreed with the proverb "The nearer the Church, the farther from God;" that he saw very plainly that the masters of the community should be its servants and not its oppressors and parasites; and that though he did not tell us not to fight our enemies, he did tell us to love them, and warned us that they who draw the sword shall perish by the sword. All this shows a great power of seeing through vulgar illusions, and a capacity for a higher morality than has yet been established in any civilized community; but it does not place Jesus above Confucius or Plato, not to mention more modern philosophers and moralists.

MARK.
THE WOMEN DISCIPLES AND THE ASCENSION.

Let us see whether we can get anything more out of Mark, whose gospel, by the way, is supposed to be older than Matthew's. Mark is brief; and it does not take long to discover that he adds nothing to Matthew except the ending of the story by Christ's ascension into heaven, and the news that many women had come with Jesus to Jerusalem, including Mary Magdalene, out of whom he had cast seven devils. On the other hand Mark says nothing about the birth of Jesus, and does not touch his career until his adult baptism by John. He apparently regards Jesus as a native of Nazareth, as John does, and not of Bethlehem, as Matthew and Luke do, Bethlehem being the city of David, from whom Jesus is said by Matthew and Luke to be descended. He describes John's doctrine as "Baptism of repentance unto remission of sins": that is, a form of Salvationism. He tells us that Jesus went into the synagogues and taught, not as the Scribes but as one having authority: that is, we infer, he preaches his own doctrine as an original moral- ist instead of repeating what the books say. He describes the miracle of Jesus reaching the boat by walking across the sea, but says nothing about Peter trying to do the same. Mark sees what he relates more vividly than Matthew, and gives touches of detail that bring the event more clearly before the reader. He says, for instance, that when Jesus walked on the waves to the boat, he was passing it by when the disciples called out to him. He seems to feel that Jesus's treatment of the woman of Canaan requires some apology, and therefore says that she was a Greek of Syrophenician race, which probably excused any incivility to her in Mark's eyes. He represents the father of the boy whom Jesus cured of epilepsy after the transfiguration as a sceptic who says "Lord, I believe: help thou mine unbelief." He tells the story of the widow's mite, omitted by Matthew. He explains that Barabbas was "lying bound with them that made insurrection, men who in the insurrection had committed murder." Joseph of Arimathea, who buried Jesus in his own tomb, and who is described by Matthew as a disciple, is described by Mark as "one who also himself was looking for the kingdom of God," which suggests that he was an independent seeker. Mark earns our gratitude by making no mention of the old prophecies, and thereby not only saves time, but avoids the absurd implication that Christ was merely going through a pre-determined ritual, like the works of a clock, instead of living. Finally Mark reports Christ as saying, after his resurrection, that those who believe in him will be saved and those who do not, damned; but it is impossible to discover whether he means anything by a state of damnation beyond a state of error. The paleographers regard this passage as tacked on by a later scribe. On the whole Mark leaves the modern reader where Matthew left him.

LUKE.
LUKE THE LITERARY ARTIST.

When we come to Luke, we come to a later storyteller, and one with a stronger natural gift for his art. Before you have read twenty lines of Luke's gospel you are aware that you have passed from the chronicler writing for the sake of recording important facts, to the artist, telling the story for the sake of telling it. At the very outset he achieves the most charming idyll in the Bible: the story of Mary crowded out of the inn into the stable and laying her newly-born son in the manger, and of the shepherds abiding in the field keeping watch over their flocks by night, and how the angel of the Lord came upon them, and the glory of the Lord shone around them, and suddenly there was with the angel a multitude of the heavenly host. These shepherds go to the stable and take the place of the kings in Matthew's chronicle. So completely has this story conquered and fascinated our imagination that most of us suppose all the gospels to contain it; but it is Luke's story and his alone: none of the others have the smallest hint of it.

THE CHARM OF LUKE'S NARRATIVE.

Luke gives the charm of sentimental romance to every incident. The Annunciation, as described by Matthew, is made to Joseph, and is simply a warning to him not to divorce his wife for misconduct. In Luke's gospel it is made to Mary herself, at much greater length, with a sense of the ecstasy of the bride of the Holy Ghost. Jesus is refined and softened almost out of recognition: the stern peremptory disciple of John the Baptist, who never addresses a Pharisee or a Scribe without an insulting epithet, becomes a considerate, gentle, sociable, almost urbane person; and the Chauvinist Jew becomes a pro-Gentile who is thrown out of the synagogue in his own town for reminding the congregation that the prophets had sometimes preferred Gentiles to Jews. In fact they try to throw him down from a sort of Tarpeian rock which they use for executions; but he makes his way through them and escapes: the only suggestion of a feat of arms on his part in the gospels. There is not a word of the Syrophenician woman. At the end he is calmly superior to his sufferings; delivers an address on his way to execution with unruffled composure; does not despair on the cross; and dies with perfect dignity, commending his spirit to God, after praying for the forgiveness of his persecutors on the ground that "They know not what they do." According to Matthew, it is part of the bitterness of his death that even the thieves who are crucified with him revile him. According to Luke, only one of them does this; and he is rebuked by the other, who begs Jesus to remember him when he comes into his kingdom. To which Jesus replies, "This day shalt thou be with me in Paradise," implying that he will spend the three days of his death there. In short, every device is used to get rid of the ruthless horror of the Matthew chronicle, and to relieve the strain of the Passion by touching episodes, and by representing Christ as superior to human suffering. It is Luke's Jesus who has won our hearts.

THE TOUCH OF PARISIAN ROMANCE.

Luke's romantic shrinking from unpleasantness, and his sentimentality, are illustrated by his version of the woman with the ointment. Matthew and Mark describe it as taking place in the house of Simon the Leper, where it is objected to as a waste of money. In Luke's version the leper becomes a rich Pharisee; the woman becomes a Dame aux Camellias; and nothing is said about money and the poor. The woman washes the feet of Jesus with her tears and dries them with her hair; and he is reproached for suffering a sinful woman to touch him. It is almost an adaptation of the unromantic Matthew to the Parisian stage. There is a distinct attempt to increase the feminine interest all through. The slight lead given by Mark is taken up and developed. More is said about Jesus's mother and her feelings. Christ's following of women, just mentioned by Mark to account for their presence at his tomb, is introduced earlier; and some of the women are named; so that we are introduced to Joanna the wife of Chuza, Herod's steward, and Susanna. There is the quaint little domestic episode between Mary and Martha. There is the parable of the Prodigal Son, appealing to the indulgence romance has always shown to Charles Surface and Des Grieux. Women follow Jesus to the cross; and he makes them a speech beginning "Daughters of Jerusalem." Slight as these changes may seem, they make a great change in the atmosphere. The Christ of Matthew could never have become what is vulgarly called a woman's hero (though the truth is that the popular demand for sentiment, as far as it is not simply human, is more manly than womanly); but the Christ of Luke has made possible those pictures which now hang in many ladies' chambers, in which Jesus is represented exactly as he is represented in the Lourdes cinematograph, by a handsome actor. The only touch of realism which Luke does not instinctively suppress for the sake of producing this kind of amenity is the reproach addressed to Jesus for sitting down to table without washing his hands; and that is retained because an interesting discourse hangs on it.

WAITING FOR THE MESSIAH.

Another new feature in Luke's story is that it begins in a world in which everyone is expecting the advent of the Christ. In Matthew and Mark, Jesus comes into a normal Philistine world like our own of today. Not until the Baptist foretells that one greater than himself shall come after him does the old Jewish hope of a Messiah begin to stir again; and as Jesus begins as a disciple of John, and is baptized by him, nobody connects him with that hope until Peter has the sudden inspiration which produces so startling an effect on Jesus. But in Luke's gospel men's minds, and especially women's minds, are full of eager expectation of a Christ not only before the birth of Jesus, but before the birth of John the Baptist, the event with which Luke begins his story. Whilst Jesus and John are still in their mothers' wombs, John leaps at the approach of Jesus when the two mothers visit one another. At the circumcision of Jesus pious men and women hail the infant as the Christ.

The Baptist himself is not convinced; for at quite a late period in his former disciple's career he sends two young men to ask Jesus is he really the Christ. This is noteworthy because Jesus immediately gives them a deliberate exhibition of miracles, and bids them tell John what they have seen, and ask him what he thinks now: This is in complete contradiction to what I have called the Rousseau view of miracles as inferred from Matthew. Luke shows all a romancer's thoughtlessness about miracles; he regards them as "signs": that is, as proofs of the divinity of the person performing them, and not merely of thaumaturgic powers. He revels in miracles just as he revels in parables: they make such capital stories. He cannot allow the calling of Peter, James, and John from their boats to pass without a comic miraculous overdraft of fishes, with the net sinking the boats and provoking Peter to exclaim, "Depart from me; for I am a sinful man, O Lord," which should probably be translated, "I want no more of your miracles: natural fishing is good enough for my boats."

There are some other novelties in Luke's version. Pilate sends Jesus to Herod, who happens to be in Jerusalem just then, because Herod had expressed some curiosity about him; but nothing comes of it: the prisoner will not speak to him. When

Jesus is ill received in a Samaritan village James and John propose to call down fire from heaven and destroy it; and Jesus replies that he is come not to destroy lives but to save them. The bias of Jesus against lawyers is emphasized, and also his resolution not to admit that he is more bound to his relatives than to strangers. He snubs a woman who blesses his mother. As this is contrary to the traditions of sentimental romance, Luke would presumably have avoided it had he not become persuaded that the brotherhood of Man and the Fatherhood of God are superior even to sentimental considerations. The story of the lawyer asking what are the two chief commandments is changed by making Jesus put the question to the lawyer instead of answering it.

As to doctrine, Luke is only clear when his feelings are touched. His logic is weak; for some of the sayings of Jesus are pieced together wrongly, as anyone who has read them in the right order and context in Matthew will discover at once. He does not make anything new out of Christ's mission, and, like the other evangelists, thinks that the whole point of it is that Jesus was the long expected Christ, and that he will presently come back to earth and establish his kingdom, having duly died and risen again after three days. Yet Luke not only records the teaching as to communism and the discarding of hate, which have, of course, nothing to do with the Second Coming, but quotes one very remarkable saying which is not compatible with it, which is, that people must not go about asking where the kingdom of heaven is, and saying "Lo, here!" and "Lo, there!" because the kingdom of heaven is within them. But Luke has no sense that this belongs to a quite different order of thought to his Christianity, and retains undisturbed his view of the kingdom as a locality as definite as Jerusalem or Madagascar.

JOHN.
A NEW STORY AND A NEW CHARACTER.

The gospel of John is a surprise after the others. Matthew, Mark and Luke describe the same events in the same order (the variations in Luke are negligible), and their gospels are therefore called the synoptic gospels. They tell substantially the same story of a wandering preacher who at the end of his life came to Jerusalem. John describes a preacher who spent practically his whole adult life in the capital, with occasional visits to the provinces. His circumstantial account of the calling of Peter and the sons of Zebedee is quite different from the others; and he says nothing about their being fishermen. He says expressly that Jesus, though baptized by John, did not himself practise baptism, and that his disciples did. Christ's agonized appeal against his doom in the garden of Gethsemane becomes a coldblooded suggestion made in the temple at a much earlier period. Jesus argues much more; complains a good deal of the unreasonableness and dislike with which he is met; is by no means silent before Caiaphas and Pilate; lays much greater stress on his resurrection and on the eating of his body (losing all his disciples except the twelve in consequence); says many apparently contradictory and nonsensical things to which no ordinary reader can now find any clue; and gives the impression of an educated, not to say sophisticated mystic, different both in character and schooling from the simple and downright preacher of Matthew and Mark, and the urbane easy-minded charmer of Luke. Indeed, the Jews say of him "How knoweth this man letters, having never learnt?"

JOHN THE IMMORTAL EYEWITNESS.

John, moreover, claims to be not only a chronicler but a witness. He declares that he is "the disciple whom Jesus loved," and that he actually leaned on the bosom of Jesus at the last supper and asked in a whisper which of them it was that should betray him. Jesus whispered that he would give a sop to the traitor, and thereupon handed one to Judas, who ate it and immediately became possessed by the devil. This is more natural than the other accounts, in which Jesus openly indicates Judas without eliciting any protest or exciting any comment. It also implies that Jesus deliberately bewitched Judas in order to bring about his own betrayal. Later on John claims that Jesus said to Peter "If I will that John tarry til I come, what is that to thee?"; and John, with a rather obvious mock modesty, adds that he must not claim to be immortal, as the disciples concluded; for Christ did not use that expression, but merely remarked "If I will that he tarry till I come." No other evangelist claims personal intimacy with Christ, or even pretends to be his contemporary (there is no ground for identifying Matthew the publican with Matthew the Evangelist); and John is the only evangelist whose account of Christ's career and character is hopelessly irreconcilable with Matthew's. He is almost as bad as Matthew, by the way, in his repeated explanations of Christ's actions as having no other purpose than to fulfil the old prophecies. The impression is more unpleasant, because, as John, unlike Matthew, is educated, subtle, and obsessed with artificial intellectual mystifications, the discovery that he is stupid or superficial in so simple a matter strikes one with distrust and dislike, in spite of his great literary charm, a good example of which is his transfiguration of the harsh episode of the Syrophenician woman into the pleasant story of the woman of Samaria. This perhaps is why his claim to be John the disciple, or to be a contemporary of Christ or even of any survivor of Christ's generation, has been disputed, and finally, it seems, disallowed. But I repeat, I take no note here of the disputes of experts as to the date of the gospels, not because I am not acquainted with them, but because, as the earliest codices are Greek manuscripts of the fourth century A.D., and the Syrian ones are translations from the Greek, the paleographic expert has no difficulty in arriving at whatever conclusion happens to suit his beliefs or disbeliefs; and he never succeeds in convincing the other experts except when they believe or disbelieve exactly as he does. Hence I conclude that the dates of the original narratives cannot be ascertained, and that we must make the best of the evangelists' own accounts of themselves. There is, as we have seen, a very marked difference between them, leaving no doubt that we are dealing with four authors of well-marked diversity; but they all end in an attitude of expectancy of the Second Coming which they agree in declaring Jesus to have positively and unequivocally promised within the lifetime of his contemporaries. Any believer compiling a gospel after the last of these contemporaries had passed away, would either reject and omit the tradition of that promise on the ground that since it was not fulfilled, and could never now be fulfilled, it could not have been made, or else have had to confess to the Jews, who were the keenest critics of the Christians, that Jesus was either an impostor or the victim of a delusion. Now all the evangelists except Matthew expressly declare themselves to be believers; and Matthew's narrative is obviously not that of a sceptic. I therefore assume as a matter of common sense that, interpolations apart, the gospels are derived from narratives written in the first century A.D. I include John, because though it may be claimed that he hedged his position by claiming that Christ, who specially loved him, endowed him with a miraculous life until the Second Coming, the conclusion being that John is alive at this moment, I cannot believe that a literary forger could hope to save the situation by so outrageous a pretension. Also, John's narrative is in many passages nearer to the realities of public life than the simple chronicle of Matthew or the sentimental romance of Luke. This may be because John was obviously more a man of the world than the others, and knew, as mere chroniclers and romancers never know, what actually happens away from books and desks. But it may also be because he saw and heard what happened instead of collecting traditions about it. The paleographers and daters of first quotations may say what they please: John's claim to give evidence as an eyewitness whilst the others are only compiling history is supported by a certain verisimilitude which appeals to me as one who has preached a new doctrine and argued about it, as well as written stories. This verisimilitude may be dramatic art backed by knowledge of public life; but even at that we must not forget that the best dramatic art is the operation of a divinatory instinct for truth. Be that as it may, John was certainly not the man to believe in the Second Coming and yet give a date for it after that date had passed. There is really no escape from the conclusion that the originals of all the gospels date from the period within which there was still a possibility of the Second Coming occurring at the promised time.

THE PECULIAR THEOLOGY OF JESUS.

In spite of the suspicions roused by John's idiosyncrasies, his narrative is of enormous importance to those who go to the gospels for a credible modern religion. For it is John who adds to the other records such sayings as that "I and my father are one"; that "God is a spirit"; that the aim of Jesus is not only that the people should have life, but that they should have it "more abundantly" (a distinction much needed by people who think a man is either alive or dead, and never consider the important question how much alive he is); and that men should bear in mind what they were told in the 82nd Psalm: that they are gods, and are responsible for the doing of the mercy and justice of God. The Jews stoned him for saying these things, and, when he remonstrated with them for stupidly stoning one who had done nothing to them but good works, replied "For a good work we stone thee not; but for blasphemy, because that thou, being a man, makest thyself God." He insists (referring to the 82nd psalm) that if it is part of their own religion that they are gods on the assurance of God himself, it cannot be blasphemy for him, whom the Father sanctified and sent into the world, to say "I am the son of God." But they will not have this at any price; and he has to escape from their fury. Here the point is obscured by the distinction made by Jesus between himself and other men. He says, in effect, "If you are gods, then, a fortiori, I am a god." John makes him say this, just as he makes him say "I am the light of the world." But Matthew makes him say to the people "Ye are the light of the world." John has no grip of the significance of these scraps which he has picked up: he is far more interested in a notion of his own that men can escape death and do even more extraordinary things than Christ himself: in fact, he actually represents Jesus as promising this explicitly, and is finally led into the audacious hint that he, John, is himself immortal in the flesh. Still, he does not miss the significant sayings altogether. However inconsistent they may be with the doctrine he is consciously driving at, they appeal to some sub-intellectual instinct in him that makes him stick them in, like a child sticking tinsel stars on the robe of a toy angel.

John does not mention the ascension; and the end of his narrative leaves Christ restored to life, and appearing from time to time among his disciples. It is on one of these occasions that John describes the miraculous draught of fishes which Luke places at the other end of Christ's career, at the call of the sons of Zebedee.

JOHN AGREED AS TO THE TRIAL AND CRUCIFIXION.

Although John, following his practice of showing Jesus's skill as a debater, makes him play a less passive part at his trial, he still gives substantially the same account of it as all the rest. And the question that would occur to any modern reader never occurs to him, any more than it occurred to Matthew, Mark, or Luke. That question is, Why on earth did not Jesus defend himself, and make the people rescue him from the High Priest? He was so popular that they were unable to prevent him driving the money-changers out of the temple, or to arrest him for it. When they did arrest him afterwards, they had to do it at night in a garden. He could have argued with them as he had often done in the temple, and justified himself both to the Jewish law and to Caesar. And he had physical force at his command to back up his arguments: all that was needed was a speech to rally his followers; and he was not gagged. The reply of the evangelists would have been that all these inquiries are idle, because if Jesus had wished to escape, he could have saved himself all that trouble by doing what John describes him as doing: that is, casting his captors to the earth by an exertion of his miraculous power. If you asked John why he let them get up again and torment and execute him, John would have replied that it was part of the destiny of God to be slain and buried and to rise again, and that to have avoided this destiny would have been to repudiate his Godhead. And that is the only apparent explanation. Whether you believe with the evangelists that Christ could have rescued himself by a miracle, or, as a modern Secularist, point out that he could have defended himself effectually, the fact remains that according to all the narratives he did not do so. He had to die like a god, not to save himself "like one of the princes."[1]

The consensus on this point is important, because it proves the absolute sincerity of Jesus's declaration that he was a god. No impostor would have accepted such dreadful consequences without an effort to save himself. No impostor would have been nerved to endure them by the conviction that he would rise from the grave and live again after three days. If we accept the story at all, we must believe this, and believe also that his promise to return in glory and establish his kingdom

---

1   Jesus himself had refered to that psalm (LXXII) in which
        men who have judged unjustly and accepted the persons of the
        wicked (including by anticipation practically all the white
        inhabitants of the British Isles and the North American
        continent, to mention no other places) are condemned in the
        words, "I have said, ye are gods; and all of ye are children
        of the Most High; but ye shall die like men, and fall like
        one of the princes."

on earth within the lifetime of men then living, was one which he believed that he could, and indeed must fulfil. Two evangelists declare that in his last agony he despaired, and reproached God for forsaking him. The other two represent him as dying in unshaken conviction and charity with the simple remark that the ordeal was finished. But all four testify that his faith was not deceived, and that he actually rose again after three days. And I think it unreasonable to doubt that all four wrote their narratives in full faith that the other promise would be fulfilled too, and that they themselves might live to witness the Second Coming.

CREDIBILITY OF THE GOSPELS.

It will be noted by the older among my readers, who are sure to be obsessed more or less by elderly wrangles as to whether the gospels are credible as matter-of-fact narratives, that I have hardly raised this question, and have accepted the credible and incredible with equal complacency. I have done this because credibility is a subjective condition, as the evolution of religious belief clearly shows. Belief is not dependent on evidence and reason. There is as much evidence that the miracles occurred as that the battle of Waterloo occurred, or that a large body of Russian troops passed through England in 1914 to take part in the war on the western front. The reasons for believing in the murder of Pompey are the same as the reasons for believing in the raising of Lazarus. Both have been believed and doubted by men of equal intelligence. Miracles, in the sense of phenomena we cannot explain, surround us on every hand; life itself is the miracle of miracles. Miracles in the sense of events that violate the normal course of our experience are vouched for every day: the flourishing Church of Christ Scientist is founded on a multitude of such miracles. Nobody believes all the miracles: everybody believes some of them. I cannot tell why men who will not believe that Jesus ever existed yet believe firmly that Shakespear was Bacon. I cannot tell why people who believe that angels appeared and fought on our side at the battle of Mons, and who believe that miracles occur quite frequently at Lourdes, nevertheless boggle at the miracle of the liquefaction of the blood of St. Januarius, and reject it as a trick of priestcraft. I cannot tell why people who will not believe Matthew's story of three kings bringing costly gifts to the cradle of Jesus, believe Luke's story of the shepherds and the stable. I cannot tell why people, brought up to believe the Bible in the old literal way as an infallible record and revelation, and rejecting that view later on, begin by rejecting the Old Testament, and give up the belief in a brimstone hell before they give up (if they ever do) the belief in a heaven of harps, crowns, and thrones. I cannot tell why people who will not believe in baptism on any terms believe in vaccination with the cruel fanaticism of inquisitors. I am convinced that if a dozen sceptics were to draw up in parallel columns a list of the events narrated in the gospels which they consider credible and incredible respectively, their lists would be different in several particulars. Belief is literally a matter of taste.

FASHIONS OF BELIEF.

Now matters of taste are mostly also matters of fashion. We are conscious of a difference between medieval fashions in belief and modern fashions. For instance, though we are more credulous than men were in the Middle Ages, and entertain such crowds of fortunetellers, magicians, miracle workers, agents of communication with the dead, discoverers of the elixir of life, transmuters of metals, and healers of all sorts, as the Middle Ages never dreamed of as possible, yet we will not take our miracles in the form that convinced the Middle Ages. Arithmetical numbers appealed to the Middle Ages just as they do to us, because they are difficult to deal with, and because the greatest masters of numbers, the Newtons and Leibnitzes, rank among the greatest men. But there are fashions in numbers too. The Middle Ages took a fancy to some familiar number like seven; and because it was an odd number, and the world was made in seven days, and there are seven stars in Charles's Wain, and for a dozen other reasons, they were ready to believe anything that had a seven or a seven times seven in it. Seven deadly sins, seven swords of sorrow in the heart of the Virgin, seven champions of Christendom, seemed obvious and reasonable things to believe in simply because they were seven. To us, on the contrary, the number seven is the stamp of superstition. We will believe in nothing less than millions. A medieval doctor gained his patient's confidence by telling him that his vitals were being devoured by seven worms. Such a diagnosis would ruin a modern physician. The modern physician tells his patient that he is ill because every drop of his blood is swarming with a million microbes; and the patient believes him abjectly and instantly. Had a bishop told William the Conqueror that the sun was seventy-seven miles distant from the earth, William would have believed him not only out of respect for the Church, but because he would have felt that seventy-seven miles was the proper distance. The Kaiser, knowing just as little about it as the Conqueror, would send that bishop to an asylum. Yet he (I presume) unhesitatingly accepts the estimate of ninety-two and nine-tenths millions of miles, or whatever the latest big figure may be.

CREDIBILITY AND TRUTH.

And here I must remind you that our credulity is not to be measured by the truth of the things we believe. When men believed that the earth was flat, they were not credulous: they were using their common sense, and, if asked to prove that the earth was flat, would have said simply, "Look at it." Those who refuse to believe that it is round are exercising a wholesome scepticism. The modern man who believes that the earth is round is grossly credulous. Flat Earth men drive him to fury by confuting him with the greatest ease when he tries to argue about it. Confront him with a theory that the earth is cylindrical, or annular, or hour-glass shaped, and he is lost. The thing he believes may be true, but that is not why he believes it: he believes it because in some mysterious way it appeals to his imagination. If you ask him why he believes that the sun is ninety-odd million miles off, either he will have to confess that he doesn't know, or he will say that Newton proved it. But he has not read the treatise in which Newton proved it, and does not even know that it was written in Latin. If you press an Ulster Protestant as to why he regards Newton as an infallible authority, and St. Thomas Aquinas or the Pope as superstitious liars whom, after his death, he will have the pleasure of watching from his place in heaven whilst they roast in eternal flame, or if you ask me why I take into serious consideration Colonel Sir Almroth Wright's estimates of the number of streptococci contained in a given volume of serum whilst I can only laugh at the earlier estimates of the number of angels that can be accommodated on the point of a needle, no reasonable reply is possible except that somehow sevens and angels are out of fashion, and billions and streptococci are all the rage. I simply cannot tell you why Bacon, Montaigne, and Cervantes had a quite different fashion of credulity and incredulity from the Venerable Bede and Piers Plowman and the divine doctors of the Aquinas-Aristotle school, who were certainly no stupider, and had the same facts before them. Still less can I explain why, if we assume that these leaders of thought had all reasoned out their beliefs, their authority seemed conclusive to one generation and blasphemous to another, neither generation having followed the reasoning or gone into the facts of the matter for itself at all.

It is therefore idle to begin disputing with the reader as to what he should believe in the gospels and what he should disbelieve. He will believe what he can, and disbelieve what he must. If he draws any lines at all, they will be quite arbitrary ones. St. John tells us that when Jesus explicitly claimed divine honors by the sacrament of his body and blood, so many of his disciples left him that their number was reduced to twelve. Many modern readers will not hold out so long: they will give in at the first miracle. Others will discriminate. They will accept the healing miracles, and reject the feeding of the multitude. To some the walking on the water will be a legendary exaggeration of a swim, ending in an ordinary rescue of Peter; and the raising of Lazarus will be only a similar glorification of a commonplace feat of artificial respiration, whilst others will scoff at it as a planned imposture in which Lazarus acted as a confederate. Between the rejection of the stories as wholly fabulous and the acceptance of them as the evangelists themselves meant them to be accepted, there will be many shades of belief and disbelief, of sympathy and derision. It is not a question of being a Christian or not. A Mahometan Arab will accept literally and without question parts of the narrative which an English Archbishop has to reject or explain away; and many Theosophists and lovers of the wisdom of India, who never enter a Christian Church except as sightseers, will revel in parts of John's gospel which mean nothing to a pious matter-of-fact Bradford manufacturer. Every reader takes from the Bible what he can get. In submitting a precis of the gospel narratives I have not implied any estimate either of their credibility or of their truth. I have simply informed him or reminded him, as the case may be, of what those narratives tell us about their hero.

CHRISTIAN ICONOLATRY AND THE PERILS OF THE ICONOCLAST.

I must now abandon this attitude, and make a serious draft on the reader's attention by facing the question whether, if and when the medieval and Methodist will-to-believe the Salvationist and miraculous side of the gospel narratives fails us, as it plainly has failed the leaders of modern thought, there will be anything left of the mission of Jesus: whether, in short, we may not throw the gospels into the waste-paper basket, or put them away on the fiction shelf of our libraries. I venture to reply that we shall be, on the contrary, in the position of the man in Bunyan's riddle who found that "the more he threw away, the more he had. "We get rid, to begin with, of the idolatrous or iconographic worship of Christ. By this I mean literally that worship which is given to pictures and statues of him, and to finished and unalterable stories about him. The test of the prevalence of this is that if you speak or write of Jesus as a real live person, or even as a still active God, such worshippers are more horrified than Don Juan was when the statue stepped from its pedestal and came to supper with him. You may deny the divinity of Jesus; you may doubt whether he ever existed; you may reject Christianity for Judaism, Mahometanism, Shintoism, or Fire Worship; and the iconolaters, placidly contemptuous, will only classify you as a freethinker or a heathen. But if you venture to wonder how Christ would have looked if he had shaved and had his hair cut, or what size in shoes he took, or whether he swore when he stood on a nail in the carpenter's shop, or could not button his robe when he was in a hurry, or whether he laughed over the repartees by which he baffled the priests when they tried to trap him into sedition and blasphemy, or even if you tell any part of his story in the vivid terms of modern colloquial slang, you will produce an extraordinary dismay and horror among the iconolaters. You will have made the picture come out of its frame, the statue descend from its pedestal, the story become real, with all the incalculable consequences that may flow from this terrifying miracle. It is at such moments that you realize that the iconolaters have never for a moment conceived Christ as a real person who meant what he said, as a fact, as a force like electricity, only needing the invention of suitable political machinery to be applied to the affairs of mankind with revolutionary effect.

Thus it is not disbelief that is dangerous in our society: it is belief. The moment it strikes you (as it may any day) that Christ is not the lifeless harmless image he has hitherto been to you, but a rallying centre for revolutionary influences which all established States and Churches fight, you must look to yourselves; for you have brought the image to life; and the mob may not be able to bear that horror.

THE ALTERNATIVE TO BARRABAS.

But mobs must be faced if civilization is to be saved. It did not need the present war to show that neither the iconographic Christ nor the Christ of St. Paul has succeeded in effecting the salvation of human society. Whilst I write, the Turks are said to be massacring the Armenian Christians on an unprecedented scale; but Europe is not in a position to remonstrate; for her Christians are slaying one another by every device which civilization has put within their reach as busily as they are slaying the Turks. Barabbas is triumphant everywhere; and the final use he makes of his triumph is to lead us all to suicide with heroic gestures and resounding lies. Now those who, like myself, see the Barabbasque social organization as a failure, and are convinced that the Life Force (or whatever you choose to call it) cannot be finally beaten by any failure, and will even supersede humanity by evolving a higher species if we cannot master the problems raised by the multiplication of our own numbers, have always known that Jesus had a real message, and have felt the fascination of his character and doctrine. Not that we should nowadays dream of claiming any supernatural authority for him, much less the technical authority which attaches to an educated modern philosopher and jurist. But when, having entirely got rid of Salvationist Christianity, and even contracted a prejudice against Jesus on the score of his involuntary connection with it, we engage on a purely scientific study of economics, criminology, and biology, and find that our practical conclusions are virtually those of Jesus, we are distinctly pleased and encouraged to find that we were doing him an injustice, and that the nimbus that surrounds his head in the pictures may be interpreted some day as a light of science rather than a declarations of sentiment or a label of idolatry.

The doctrines in which Jesus is thus confirmed are, roughly, the following:

1. The kingdom of heaven is within you. You are the son of God; and God is the son of man. God is a spirit, to be worshipped in spirit and in truth, and not an elderly gentleman to be bribed and begged from. We are members one of another; so that you cannot injure or help your neighbor without injuring or helping yourself. God is your father: you are here to do God's work; and you and your father are one.

2. Get rid of property by throwing it into the common stock. Dissociate your work entirely from money payments. If you let a child starve you are letting God starve. Get rid of all anxiety about tomorrow's dinner and clothes, because you cannot serve two masters: God and Mammon.

S. Get rid of judges and punishment and revenge. Love your neighbor as yourself, he being a part of yourself. And love your enemies: they are your neighbors.

4. Get rid of your family entanglements. Every mother you meet is as much your mother as the woman who bore you. Every man you meet is as much your brother as the man she bore after you. Don't waste your time at family funerals grieving for your relatives: attend to life, not to death: there are as good fish in the sea as ever came out of it, and better. In the kingdom of heaven, which, as aforesaid, is within you, there is no marriage nor giving in marriage, because you cannot devote your life to two divinities: God and the person you are married to.

Now these are very interesting propositions; and they become more interesting every day, as experience and science drive us more and more to consider them favorably. In considering them, we shall waste our time unless we give them a reasonable construction. We must assume that the man who saw his way through such a mass of popular passion and illusion as stands between us and a sense of the value of such teaching was quite aware of all the objections that occur to an average stockbroker in the first five minutes. It is true that the world is governed to a considerable extent by the considerations that occur to stockbrokers in the first five minutes; but as the result is that the world is so badly governed that those who know the truth can hardly bear to live in it, an objection from an average stockbroker constitutes in itself a prima facie case for any social reform.

THE REDUCTION TO MODERN PRACTICE OF CHRISTIANITY.

All the same, we must reduce the ethical counsels and proposals of Jesus to modern practice if they are to be of any use to us. If we ask our stockbroker to act simply as Jesus advised his disciples to act, he will reply, very justly, "You are advising me to become a tramp." If we urge a rich man to sell all that he has and give it to the poor, he will inform us that such an operation is impossible. If he sells his shares and his lands, their purchaser will continue all those activities which oppress the poor. If all the rich men take the advice simultaneously the shares will fall to zero and the lands be unsaleable. If one man sells out and throws the money into the slums, the only result will be to add himself and his dependents to the list of the poor, and to do no good to the poor beyond giving a chance few of them a drunken spree. We must therefore bear in mind that whereas, in the time of Jesus, and in the ages which grew darker and darker after his death until the darkness, after a brief false dawn in the Reformation and the Renascence, culminated in the commercial night of the nineteenth century, it was believed that you could not make men good by Act of Parliament, we now know that you cannot make them good in any other way, and that a man who is better than his fellows is a nuisance. The rich man must sell up not only himself but his whole class; and that can be done only through the Chancellor of the Exchequer. The dis- ciple cannot have his bread without money until there is bread for everybody without money; and that requires an elaborate municipal organization of the food supply, rate supported. Being members one of another means One Man One Vote, and One Woman One Vote, and universal suffrage and equal incomes and all sorts of modern political measures. Even in Syria in the time of Jesus his teachings could not possibly have been realized by a series of independent explosions of personal righteousness on the part of the separate units of the population. Jerusalem could not have done what even a village community cannot do, and what Robinson Crusoe himself could not have done if his conscience, and the stern compulsion of Nature, had not imposed a common rule on the half dozen Robinson Crusoes who struggled within him for not wholly compatible satisfactions. And what cannot be done in Jerusalem or Juan Fernandez cannot be done in London, New York, Paris, and Berlin. In short, Christianity, good or bad, right or wrong, must perforce be left out of the question in human affairs until it is made practically applicable to them by complicated political devices; and to pretend that a field preacher under the governorship of Pontius Pilate, or even Pontius Pilate himself in council with all the wisdom of Rome, could have worked out applications of Christianity or any other system of morals for the twentieth century, is to shelve the subject much more effectually than Nero and all its other persecutors ever succeeded in doing. Personal righteousness, and the view that you cannot make people moral by Act of Parliament, is, in fact, the favorite defensive resort of the people who, consciously or subconsciously, are quite determined not to have their property meddled with by Jesus or any other reformer.

MODERN COMMUNISM.

Now let us see what modern experience and modern sociology has to say to the teaching of Jesus as summarized here. First, get rid of your property by throwing it into the common stock. One can hear the Pharisees of Jerusalem and Chorazin and Bethsaida saying, "My good fellow, if you were to divide up the wealth of Judea equally today, before the end of the year you would have rich and poor, poverty and affluence, just as you have today; for there will always be the idle and the industrious, the thrifty and the wasteful, the drunken and the sober; and, as you yourself have very justly observed, the poor we shall have always with us." And we can hear the reply, "Woe unto you, liars and hypocrites; for ye have this very day divided up the wealth of the country yourselves, as must be done every day (for man liveth not otherwise than from hand to mouth, nor can fish and eggs endure for ever); and ye have divided it unjustly; also ye have said that my reproach to you for having the poor always with you was a law unto you that this evil should persist and stink in the nostrils of God to all eternity; wherefore I think that Lazarus will yet see you beside Dives in hell." Modern Capitalism has made short work of the primitive pleas for inequality. The Pharisees themselves have organized communism in capital. Joint stock is the order of the day. An attempt to return to individual properties as the basis of our production would smash civilization more completely than ten revolutions. You cannot get the fields tilled today until the farmer becomes a co-operator. Take the shareholder to his railway, and ask him to point out to you the particular length of rail, the particular seat in the railway carriage, the particular lever in the engine that is his very own and nobody else's; and he will shun you as a madman, very wisely. And if, like Ananias and Sapphira, you try to hold back your little shop or what not from the common stock, represented by the Trust, or Combine, or Kartel, the Trust will presently freeze you out and rope you in and finally strike you dead industrially as thoroughly as St. Peter himself. There is no longer any practical question open as to Communism in production: the struggle today is over the distribution of the product: that is, over the daily dividing-up which is the first necessity of organized society.

REDISTRIBUTION.

Now it needs no Christ to convince anybody today that our system of distribution is wildly and monstrously wrong. We have million-dollar babies side by side with paupers worn out by a long life of unremitted drudgery. One person in every five dies in a workhouse, a public hospital, or a madhouse. In cities like London the proportion is very nearly one in two. Naturally so outrageous a distribution has to be effected by violence pure and simple. If you demur, you are sold up. If you resist the selling up you are bludgeoned and imprisoned, the process being euphemistically called the maintenance of law and order. Iniquity can go no further. By this time nobody who knows the figures of the distribution defends them. The most bigoted British Conservative hesitates to say that his king should be much poorer than Mr. Rockefeller, or to proclaim the moral superiority of prostitution to needlework on the ground that it pays better. The need for a drastic redistribution of income in all civilized countries is now as obvious and as generally admitted as the need for sanitation.

SHALL HE WHO MAKES, OWN.

It is when we come to the question of the proportions in which we are to redistribute that controversy begins. We are bewildered by an absurdly unpractical notion that in some way a man's income should be given to him, not to enable him to live, but as a sort of Sunday School Prize for good behavior. And this folly is complicated by a less ridiculous but quite as unpractical belief that it is possible to assign to each person the exact portion of the national income that he or she has produced. To a child it seems that the blacksmith has made a horse-shoe, and that therefore the horse-shoe is his. But the blacksmith knows that the horse-shoe does not belong solely to him, but to his landlord, to the rate collector and taxgatherer, to the men from whom he bought the iron and anvil and the coals, leaving only a scrap of its value for himself; and this scrap he has to exchange with the butcher and baker and the clothier for the things that he really appropriates as living tissue or its wrappings, paying for all of them more than their cost; for these fellow traders of his have also their landlords and moneylenders to satisfy. If, then, such simple and direct village examples of apparent individual production turn out on a moment's examination to be the products of an elaborate social organization, what is to be said of such products as dreadnoughts, factory-made pins and needles, and steel pens? If God takes the dreadnought in one hand and a steel pen in the other, and asks Job who made them, and to whom they should belong by maker's right, Job must scratch his puzzled head with a potsherd and be dumb, unless indeed it strikes him that God is the ultimate maker, and that all we have a right to do with the product is to feed his lambs.

LABOR TIME.

So maker's right as an alternative to taking the advice of Jesus would not work. In practice nothing was possible in that direction but to pay a worker by labor time so much an hour or day or week or year. But how much? When that question came up, the only answer was "as little as he can be starved into accepting," with the ridiculous results already mentioned, and the additional anomaly that the largest share went to the people who did not work at all, and the least to those who worked hardest. In England nine-tenths of the wealth goes into the pockets of one-tenth of the population.

THE DREAM OF DISTRIBUTION ACCORDING TO MERIT.

Against this comes the protest of the Sunday School theorists "Why not distribute according to merit?" Here one imagines Jesus, whose smile has been broadening down the ages as attempt after attempt to escape from his teaching has led to deeper and deeper disaster, laughing outright. Was ever so idiotic a project mooted as the estimation of virtue in money? The London School of Economics is, we must suppose, to set examination papers with such questions as, "Taking the money value of the virtues of Jesus as 100, and of Judas Iscariot as zero, give the correct figures for, respectively, Pontius Pilate, the proprietor of the Gadarene swine, the widow who put her mite in the poor-box, Mr. Horatio Bottomley, Shakespear, Mr. Jack Johnson, Sir Isaac Newton, Palestrina, Offenbach, Sir Thomas Lipton, Mr. Paul Cinquevalli, your family doctor, Florence Nightingale, Mrs. Siddons, your charwoman, the Archbishop of Canterbury, and the common hangman." Or "The late Mr. Barney Barnato received as his lawful income three thousand times as much money as an English agricultural laborer of good general character. Name the principal virtues in which Mr. Barnato exceeded the laborer three thousandfold; and give in figures the loss sustained by civilization when Mr. Barnato was driven to despair and suicide by the reduction of his multiple to one thousand." The Sunday School idea, with its principle "to each the income he deserves" is really too silly for discussion. Hamlet disposed of it three hundred years ago. "Use every man after his deserts, and who shall scape whipping?" Jesus remains unshaken as the practical man; and we stand exposed as the fools, the blunderers, the unpractical visionaries. The moment you try to reduce the Sunday School idea to figures you find that it brings you back to the hopeless plan of paying for a man's time; and your examination paper will read

"The time of Jesus was worth nothing (he complained that the foxes had holes and the birds of the air nests whilst he had not a place to lay his head). Dr. Crippen's time was worth, say, three hundred and fifty pounds a year. Criticize this arrangement; and, if you dispute its justice, state in pounds, dollars, francs and marks, what their relative time wages ought to have been." Your answer may be that the question is in extremely bad taste and that you decline to answer it. But you cannot object to being asked how many minutes of a bookmaker's time is worth two hours of an astronomer's?

VITAL DISTRIBUTION.

In the end you are forced to ask the question you should have asked at the beginning. What do you give a man an income for? Obviously to keep him alive. Since it is evident that the first condition on which he can be kept alive without enslaving somebody else is that he shall produce an equivalent for what it costs to keep him alive, we may quite rationally compel him to abstain from idling by whatever means we employ to compel him to abstain from murder, arson, forgery, or any other crime. The one supremely foolish thing to do with him is to do nothing; that is, to be as idle, lazy, and heartless in dealing with him as he is in dealing with us. Even if we provided work for him instead of basing, as we do, our whole industrial system on successive competitive waves of overwork with their ensuing troughs of unemployment, we should still sternly deny him the alternative of not doing it; for the result must be that he will become poor and make his children poor if he has any; and poor people are cancers in the commonwealth, costing far more than if they were handsomely pensioned off as incurables. Jesus had more sense than to propose anything of the sort. He said to his disciples, in effect, "Do your work for love; and let the other people lodge and feed and clothe you for love." Or, as we should put it nowadays, "for nothing." All human experience and all natural uncommercialized human aspiration point to this as the right path. The Greeks said, "First secure an independent income; and then practise virtue." We all strive towards an independent income. We all know as well as Jesus did that if we have to take thought for the morrow as to whether there shall be anything to eat or drink it will be impossible for us to think of nobler things, or live a higher life than that of a mole, whose life is from beginning to end a frenzied pursuit of food. Until the community is organized in such a way that the fear of bodily want is forgotten as completely as the fear of wolves already is in civilized capitals, we shall never have a decent social life. Indeed the whole attraction of our present arrangements lies in the fact that they do relieve a handful of us from this fear; but as the relief is effected stupidly and wickedly by making the favored handful parasitic on the rest, they are smitten with the degeneracy which seems to be the inevitable biological penalty of complete parasitism, and corrupt culture and statecraft instead of contributing to them, their excessive leisure being as mischievous as the excessive toil of the laborers. Anyhow, the moral is clear. The two main problems of organized society, how to secure the subsistence of all its members, and how to prevent the theft of that subsistence by idlers, should be entirely dissociated; and the practical failure of one of them to automatically achieve the other recognized and acted on. We may not all have Jesus's psychological power of seeing, without any enlightenment from more modern economic phenomena, that they must fail; but we have the hard fact before us that they do fail. The only people who cling to the lazy delusion that it is possible to find a just distribution that will work automatically are those who postulate some revolutionary change like land nationalization, which by itself would obviously only force into greater urgency the problem of how to distribute the product of the land among all the individuals in the community.

EQUAL DISTRIBUTION.

When that problem is at last faced, the question of the proportion in which the national income shall be distributed can have only one answer. All our shares must be equal. It has always been so; it always will be so. It is true that the incomes of robbers vary considerably from individual to individual; and the variation is reflected in the incomes of their parasites. The commercialization of certain exceptional talents has also produced exceptional incomes, direct and derivative. Persons who live on rent of land and capital are economically, though not legally, in the category of robbers, and have grotesquely different incomes. But in the huge mass of mankind variation Of income from individual to individual is unknown, because it is ridiculously impracticable. As a device for persuading a carpenter that a judge is a creature of superior nature to himself, to be deferred and submitted to even to the death, we may give a carpenter a hundred pounds a year and a judge five thousand; but the wage for one carpenter is the wage for all the carpenters: the salary for one judge is the salary for all the judges.

THE CAPTAIN AND THE CABIN BOY.

Nothing, therefore, is really in question, or ever has been, but the differences between class incomes. Already there is economic equality between captains, and economic equality between cabin boys. What is at issue still is whether there shall be economic equality between captains and cabin boys. What would Jesus have said? Presumably he would have said that if your only object is to produce a captain and a cabin boy for the purpose of transferring you from Liverpool to New York, or to manoeuvre a fleet and carry powder from the magazine to the gun, then you need give no more than a shilling to the cabin boy for every pound you give to the more expensively trained captain. But if in addition to this you desire to allow the two human souls which are inseparable from the captain and the cabin boy, and which alone differentiate them from the donkey-engine, to develop all their possibilities, then you may find the cabin boy costing rather more than the captain, because cabin boy's work does not do so much for the soul as captain's work. Consequently you will have to give him at least as much as the captain unless you definitely wish him to be a lower creature, in which case the sooner you are hanged as an abortion-ist the better. That is the fundamental argument.

THE POLITICAL AND BIOLOGICAL OBJECTIONS TO INEQUALITY.

But there are other reasons for objecting to class stratification of income which have heaped themselves up since the time of Jesus. In politics it defeats every form of government except that of a necessarily corrupt oligarchy. Democracy in the most democratic modern republics: Prance and the United States for example, is an imposture and a delusion. It reduces justice and law to a farce: law becomes merely an instrument for keeping the poor in subjection; and accused workmen are tried, not by a jury of their peers, but by conspiracies of their exploiters. The press is the press of the rich and the curse of the poor: it becomes dangerous to teach men to read. The priest becomes the mere complement of the policeman in the machinery by which the countryhouse oppresses the village. Worst of all, marriage becomes a class affair: the infinite variety of choice which nature offers to the young in search of a mate is narrowed to a handful of persons of similar income; and beauty and health become the dreams of artists and the advertisements of quacks instead of the normal conditions of life. Society is not only divided but actually destroyed in all directions by inequality of income between classes: such stability as it has is due to the huge blocks of people between whom there is equality of income.

JESUS AS ECONOMIST.   It seems therefore that we must begin by holding the right to an income as sacred and equal, just as we now begin by holding the right to life as sacred and equal. Indeed the one right is only a restatement of the other. To hang me for cutting a dock laborer's throat after making much of me for leaving him to starve when I do not happen to have a ship for him to unload is idiotic; for as he does far less mischief with his throat cut than when he is starving, a rational society would esteem the cutthroat more highly than the capitalist. The thing has become so obvious, and the evil so unendurable, that if our attempt at civilization is not to perish like all the previous ones, we shall have to organize our society in such a way as to be able to say to every person in the land, "Take no thought, saying What shall we eat? or What shall we drink? or Wherewithal shall we be clothed?" We shall then no longer have a race of men whose hearts are in their pockets and safes and at their bankers. As Jesus said, where your treasure is, there will your heart be also. That was why he recommended that money should cease to be a treasure, and that we should take steps to make ourselves utterly reckless of it, setting our minds free for higher uses. In other words, that we should all be gentlemen and take care of our country because our country takes care of us, instead of the commercialized cads we are, doing everything and anything for money, and selling our souls and bodies by the pound and the inch after wasting half the day haggling over the price. Decidedly, whether you think Jesus was God or not, you must admit that he was a first-rate political economist.

JESUS AS BIOLOGIST.

He was also, as we now see, a first-rate biologist. It took a century and a half of evolutionary preachers, from Buffon and Goethe to Butler and Bergson, to convince us that we and our father are one; that as the kingdom of heaven is within us we need not go about looking for it and crying Lo here! and Lo there!; that God is not a picture of a pompous person in white robes in the family Bible, but a spirit; that it is through this spirit that we evolve towards greater abundance of life; that we are the lamps in which the light of the world burns: that, in cohort, we are gods though we die like men. All that is today sound biology and psychology; and the efforts of Natural Selectionists like Weismann to reduce evolution to mere automatism have not touched the doctrine of Jesus, though they have made short work of the theologians who conceived God as a magnate keeping men and angels as Lord Rothschild keeps buffaloes and emus at Tring.

MONEY THE MIDWIFE OF SCIENTIFIC COMMUNISM.

It may be asked here by some simple-minded reader why we should not resort to crude Communism as the disciples were told to do. This would be quite practicable in a village where production was limited to the supply of the primitive wants which nature imposes on all human beings alike. We know that people need bread and boots without waiting for them to come and ask for these things and offer to pay for them. But when civilization advances to the point at which articles are produced that no man absolutely needs and that only some men fancy or can use, it is necessary that individuals should be able to have things made to their order and at their own cost. It is safe to provide bread for everybody because everybody wants and eats bread; but it would be absurd to provide microscopes and trombones, pet snakes and polo mallets, alembics and test tubes for everybody, as nine-tenths of them would be wasted; and the nine-tenths of the population who do not use such things would object to their being provided at all. We have in the invaluable instrument called money a means of enabling every individual to order and pay for the particular things he desires over and above the things he must consume in order to remain alive, plus the things the State insists on his having and using whether he wants to or not; for example, clothes, sanitary arrangements, armies and navies. In large communities, where even the most eccentric demands for manufactured articles average themselves out until they can be foreseen within a negligible margin of error, direct communism (Take what you want without payment, as the people do in Morris's News From Nowhere) will, after a little experience, be found not only practicable but highly economical to an extent that now seems impossible. The sportsmen, the musicians, the physicists, the biologists will get their apparatus for the asking as easily as their bread, or, as at present, their paving, street lighting, and bridges; and the deaf man will not object to contribute to communal flutes when the musician has to contribute to communal ear trumpets. There are cases (for example, radium) in which the demand may be limited to the merest handful of laboratory workers, and in which nevertheless the whole community must pay because the price is beyond the means of any individual worker. But even when the utmost allowance is made for extensions of communism that now seem fabulous, there will still remain for a long time to come regions of supply and demand in which men will need and use money or individual credit, and for which, therefore, they must have individual incomes. Foreign travel is an obvious instance. We are so far from even national communism still, that we shall probably have considerable developments of local communism before it becomes possible for a Manchester man to go up to London for a day without taking any money with him. The modern practical form of the communism of Jesus is therefore, for the present, equal distribution of the surplus of the national income that is not absorbed by simple communism.

JUDGE NOT.

In dealing with crime and the family, modern thought and experience have thrown no fresh light on the views of Jesus. When Swift had occasion to illustrate the corruption of our civilization by making a catalogue of the types of scoundrels it produces, he always gave judges a conspicuous place alongside of them they judged. And he seems to have done this not as a restatement of the doctrine of Jesus, but as the outcome of his own observation and judgment. One of Mr. Gilbert Chesterton's stories has for its hero a judge who, whilst trying a criminal case, is so overwhelmed by the absurdity of his position and the wickedness of the things it forces him to do, that he throws off the ermine there and then, and goes out into the world to live the life of an honest man instead of that of a cruel idol. There has also been a propaganda of a soulless stupidity called Determinism, representing man as a dead object driven hither and thither by his environment, antecedents, circumstances, and so forth, which nevertheless does remind us that there are limits to the number of cubits an individual can add to his stature morally or physically, and that it is silly as well as cruel to torment a man five feet high for not being able to pluck fruit that is within the reach of men of average height. I have known a case of an unfortunate child being beaten for not being able to tell the time after receiving an elaborate explanation of the figures on a clock dial, the fact being that she was short-sighted and could not see them. This is a typical illustration of the absurdities and cruelties into which we are led by the counter-stupidity to Determinism: the doctrine of Free Will. The notion that people can be good if they like, and that you should give them a powerful additional motive for goodness by tormenting them when they do evil, would soon reduce itself to absurdity if its application were not kept within the limits which nature sets to the self-control of most of us. Nobody supposes that a man with no ear for music or no mathematical faculty could be compelled on pain of death, however cruelly inflicted, to hum all the themes of Beethoven's symphonies or to complete Newton's work on fluxions.

LIMITS TO FREE WILL.

Consequently such of our laws as are not merely the intimidations by which tyrannies are maintained under pretext of law, can be obeyed through the exercise of a quite common degree of reasoning power and self-control. Most men and women can endure the ordinary annoyances and disappointments of life without committing murderous assaults. They conclude therefore that any person can refrain from such assaults if he or she chooses to, and proceed to reinforce self-control by threats of severe punishment. But in this they are mistaken. There are people, some of them possessing considerable powers of mind and body, who can no more restrain the fury into which a trifling mishap throws them than a dog can restrain himself from snapping if he is suddenly and painfully pinched. People fling knives and lighted paraffin lamps at one another in a dispute over a dinner-table. Men who have suffered several long sentences of penal servitude for murderous assaults will, the very day after they are released, seize their wives and cast them under drays at an irritating word. We have not only people who cannot resist an opportunity of stealing for the sake of satisfying their wants, but even people who have a specific mania for stealing, and do it when they are in no need of the things they steal. Burglary fascinates some men as sailoring fascinates some boys. Among respectable people how many are there who can be restrained by the warnings of their doctors and the lessons of experience from eating and drinking more than is good for them? It is true that between self-controlled people and ungovernable people there is a narrow margin of moral malingerers who can be made to behave themselves by the fear of consequences; but it is not worth while maintaining an abominable system of malicious, deliberate, costly and degrading ill-treatment of criminals for the sake of these marginal cases. For practical dealing with crime, Determinism or Predestination is quite a good working rule. People without self-control enough for social purposes may be killed, or may be kept in asylums with a view to studying their condition and ascertaining whether it is curable. To torture them and give ourselves virtuous airs at their expense is ridiculous and barbarous; and the desire to do it is vindictive and cruel. And though vindictiveness and cruelty are at least human qualities when they are frankly proclaimed and indulged, they are loathsome when they assume the robes of Justice. Which, I take it, is why Shakespear's Isabella gave such a dressing-down to Judge Angelo, and why Swift reserved the hottest corner of his hell for judges. Also, of course, why Jesus said "Judge not that ye be not judged" and "If any man hear my words and believe not, I judge him not" because "he hath one that judgeth him": namely, the Father who is one with him.

When we are robbed we generally appeal to the criminal law, not considering that if the criminal law were effective we should not have been robbed. That convicts us of vengeance.

I need not elaborate the argument further. I have dealt with it sufficiently elsewhere. I have only to point out that we have been judging and punishing ever since Jesus told us not to; and I defy anyone to make out a convincing case for believing that the world has been any better than it would have been if there had never been a judge, a prison, or a gallows in it all that time. We have simply added the misery of punishment to the misery of crime, and the cruelty of the judge to the cruelty of the criminal. We have taken the bad man, and made him worse by torture and degradation, incidentally making ourselves worse in the process. It does not seem very sensible, does it? It would have been far easier to kill him as kindly as possible, or to label him and leave him to his conscience, or to treat him as an invalid or a lunatic is now treated (it is only of late years, by the way, that madmen have been delivered from the whip, the chain, and the cage; and this, I presume, is the form in which the teaching of Jesus could have been put into practice.)

JESUS ON MARRIAGE AND THE FAMILY.

When we come to marriage and the family, we find Jesus making the same objection to that individual appropriation of human beings which is the essence of matrimony as to the individual appropriation of wealth. A married man, he said, will try to please his wife, and a married woman to please her husband, instead of doing the work of God. This is another version of "Where your treasure is, there will your heart be also." Eighteen hundred years later we find a very different person from Jesus, Talleyrand to wit, saying the same thing. A married man with a family, said Talleyrand, will do anything for money. Now this, though not a scientifically precise statement, is true enough to be a moral objection to marriage. As long as a man has a right to risk his life or his livelihood for his ideas he needs only courage and conviction to make his integrity unassailable. But he forfeits that right when he marries. It took a revolution to rescue Wagner from his Court appointment at Dresden; and his wife never forgave him for being glad and feeling free when he lost it and threw her back into poverty. Millet might have gone on painting potboiling nudes to the end of his life if his wife had not been of a heroic turn herself. Women, for the sake of their children and parents, submit to slaveries and prostitutions that no unattached woman would endure.

This was the beginning and the end of the objection of Jesus to marriage and family ties, and the explanation of his conception of heaven as a place where there should be neither marrying nor giving in marriage. Now there is no reason to suppose that when he said this he did not mean it. He did not, as St. Paul did afterwards in his name, propose celibacy as a rule of life; for he was not a fool, nor, when he denounced marriage, had he yet come to believe, as St. Paul did, that the end of the world was at hand and there was therefore no more need to replenish the earth. He must have meant that the race should be continued without dividing with women and men the allegiance the individual owes to God within him. This raises the practical problem of how we are to secure the spiritual freedom and integrity of the priest and the nun without their barrenness and uncompleted experience. Luther the priest did not solve the problem by marrying a nun: he only testified in the most convincing and practical way to the fact that celibacy was a worse failure than marriage.

WHY JESUS DID NOT MARRY.

To all appearance the problem oppresses only a few exceptional people. Thoroughly conventional women married to thoroughly conventional men should not be conscious of any restriction: the chain not only leaves them free to do whatever they want to do, but greatly facilitates their doing it. To them an attack on marriage is not a blow struck in defence of their freedom but at their rights and privileges. One would expect that they would not only demur vehemently to the teachings of Jesus in this matter, but object strongly to his not having been a married man himself. Even those who regard him as a god descended from his throne in heaven to take on humanity for a time might reasonably declare that the assumption of humanity must have been incomplete at its most vital point if he were a celibate. But the facts are flatly contrary. The mere thought of Jesus as a married man is felt to be blasphemous by the most conventional believers; and even those of us to whom

Jesus is no supernatural personage, but a prophet only as Mahomet was a prophet, feel that there was something more dignified in the bachelordom of Jesus than in the spectacle of Mahomet lying distracted on the floor of his harem whilst his wives stormed and squabbled and henpecked round him. We are not surprised that when Jesus called the sons of Zebedee to follow him, he did not call their father, and that the disciples, like Jesus himself, were all men without family entanglements. It is evident from his impatience when people excused themselves from following him because of their family funerals, or when they assumed that his first duty was to his mother, that he had found family ties and domestic affections in his way at every turn, and had become persuaded at last that no man could follow his inner light until he was free from their compulsion. The absence of any protest against this tempts us to declare on this question of marriage there are no conventional people; and that everyone of us is at heart a good Christian sexually.

INCONSISTENCY OF THE SEX INSTINCT.

But the question is not so simple as that. Sex is an exceedingly subtle and complicated instinct; and the mass of mankind neither know nor care much about freedom of conscience, which is what Jesus was thinking about, and are concerned almost to obsession with sex, as to which Jesus said nothing. In our sexual natures we are torn by an irresistible attraction and an overwhelming repugnance and disgust. We have two tyrannous physical passions: concupiscence and chastity. We become mad in pursuit of sex: we become equally mad in the persecution of that pursuit. Unless we gratify our desire the race is lost: unless we restrain it we destroy ourselves. We are thus led to devise marriage institutions which will at the same time secure opportunities for the gratification of sex and raise up innumerable obstacles to it; which will sanctify it and brand it as infamous; which will identify it with virtue and with sin simultaneously. Obviously it is useless to look for any consistency in such institutions; and it is only by continual reform and readjustment, and by a considerable elasticity in their enforcement, that a tolerable result can be arrived at. I need not repeat here the long and elaborate examination of them that I prefixed to my play entitled Getting Married. Here I am concerned only with the views of Jesus on the question; and it is necessary, in order to understand the attitude of the world towards them, that we should not attribute the general approval of the decision of Jesus to remain unmarried as an endorsement of his views. We are simply in a state of confusion on the subject; but it is part of the confusion that we should conclude that Jesus was a celibate, and shrink even from the idea that his birth was a natural one, yet cling with ferocity to the sacredness of the institution which provides a refuge from celibacy.

FOR BETTER OR WORSE.

Jesus, however, did not express a complicated view of marriage. His objection to it was quite simple, as we have seen. He perceived that nobody could live the higher life unless money and sexual love were obtainable without sacrificing it; and he saw that the effect of marriage as it existed among the Jews (and as it still exists among ourselves) was to make the couples sacrifice every higher consideration until they had fed and pleased one another. The worst of it is that this dangerous preposterousness in marriage, instead of improving as the general conduct of married couples improves, becomes much worse. The selfish man to whom his wife is nothing but a slave, the selfish woman to whom her husband is nothing but a scapegoat and a breadwinner, are not held back from spiritual or any other adventures by fear of their effect on the welfare of their mates. Their wives do not make recreants and cowards of them: their husbands do not chain them to the cradle and the cooking range when their feet should be beautiful on the mountains. It is precisely as people become more kindly, more conscientious, more ready to shoulder the heavier part of the burden (which means that the strong shall give way to the weak and the slow hold back the swift), that marriage becomes an intolerable obstacle to individual evolution. And that is why the revolt against marriage of which Jesus was an exponent always recurs when civilization raises the standard of marital duty and affection, and at the same time produces a greater need for individual freedom in pursuit of a higher evolution. This, fortunately, is only one side of marriage; and the question arises, can it not be eliminated? The reply is reassuring: of course it can. There is no mortal reason in the nature of things why a married couple should be economically dependent on one another. The Communism advocated by Jesus, which we have seen to be entirely practicable, and indeed inevitable if our civilization is to be saved from collapse, gets rid of that difficulty completely. And with the economic dependence will go the force of the outrageous claims that derive their real sanction from the economic pressure behind them. When a man allows his wife to turn him from the best work he is capable of doing, and to sell his soul at the highest commercial prices obtainable; when he allows her to entangle him in a social routine that is wearisome and debilitating to him, or tie him to her apron strings when he needs that occasional solitude which is one of the most sacred of human rights, he does so because he has no right to impose eccentric standards of expenditure and unsocial habits on her, and because these conditions have produced by their pressure so general a custom of chaining wedded couples to one another that married people are coarsely derided when their partners break the chain. And when a woman is condemned by her parents to wait in genteel idleness and uselessness for a husband when all her healthy social instincts call her to acquire a profession and work, it is again her economic dependence on them that makes their tyranny effective.

THE CASE FOR MARRIAGE.

Thus, though it would be too much to say that everything that is obnoxious in marriage and family life will be cured by Communism, yet it can be said that it will cure what Jesus objected to in these institutions. He made no comprehensive study of them: he only expressed his own grievance with an overwhelming sense that it is a grievance so deep that all the considerations on the other side are as dust in the balance. Obviously there are such considerations, and very weighty ones too. When Talleyrand said that a married man with a family is capable of anything, he meant anything evil; but an optimist may declare, with equal half truth, that a married man is capable of anything good; that marriage turns vagabonds into steady citizens; and that men and women will, for love of their mates and children, practise virtues that unattached individuals are incapable of. It is true that too much of this domestic virtue is self-denial, which is not a virtue at all; but then the following of the inner light at all costs is largely self-indulgence, which is just as suicidal, just as weak, just as cowardly as self-denial. Ibsen, who takes us into the matter far more resolutely than Jesus, is unable to find any golden rule: both Brand and Peer Gynt come to a bad end; and though Brand does not do as much mischief as Peer, the mischief he does do is of extraordinary intensity.

CELIBACY NO REMEDY.

We must, I think, regard the protest of Jesus against marriage and family ties as the claim of a particular kind of individual to be free from them because they hamper his own work intolerably. When he said that if we are to follow him in the sense of taking up his work we must give up our family ties, he was simply stating a fact; and to this day the Roman Catholic priest, the Buddhist lama, and the fakirs of all the eastern denominations accept the saying. It is also accepted by the physically enterprising, the explorers, the restlessly energetic of all kinds, in short, by the adventurous. The greatest sacrifice in marriage is the sacrifice of the adventurous attitude towards life: the being settled. Those who are born tired may crave for settlement; but to fresher and stronger spirits it is a form of suicide. Now to say of any institution that it is incompatible with both the contemplative and adventurous life is to disgrace it so vitally that all the moralizings of all the Deans and Chapters cannot reconcile our souls to its slavery. The unmarried Jesus and the unmarried Beethoven, the unmarried Joan of Arc, Clare, Teresa, Florence Nightingale seem as they should be; and the saying that there is always something ridiculous about a married philosopher becomes inevitable. And yet the celibate is still more ridiculous than the married man: the priest, in accepting the alternative of celibacy, disables himself; and the best priests are those who have been men of this world before they became men of the world to come. But as the taking of vows does not annul an existing marriage, and a married man cannot become a priest, we are again confronted with the absurdity that the best priest is a reformed rake. Thus does marriage, itself intolerable, thrust us upon intolerable alternatives. The practical solution is to make the individual economically independent of marriage and the family, and to make marriage as easily dissoluble as any other partnership: in other words, to accept the conclusions to which experience is slowly driving both our sociologists and our legislators. This will not instantly cure all the evils of marriage, nor root up at one stroke its detestable tradition of property in human bodies. But it will leave Nature free to effect a cure; and in free soil the root may wither and perish.

This disposes of all the opinions and teachings of Jesus which are still matters of controversy. They are all in line with the best modern thought. He told us what we have to do; and we have had to find the way to do it. Most of us are still, as most were in his own time, extremely recalcitrant, and are being forced along that way by painful pressure of circumstances, protesting at every step that nothing will induce us to go; that it is a ridiculous way, a disgraceful way, a socialistic way, an atheistic way, an immoral way, and that the vanguard ought to be ashamed of themselves and must be made to turn back at once. But they find that they have to follow the vanguard all the same if their lives are to be worth living.

AFTER THE CRUCIFIXION.

Let us now return to the New Testament narrative; for what happened after the disappearance of Jesus is instructive. Unfortunately, the crucifixion was a complete political success. I remember that when I described it in these terms once before, I greatly shocked a most respectable newspaper in my native town, the Dublin Daily Express, because my journalistic phrase showed that I was treating it as an ordinary event like Home Rule or the Insurance Act: that is (though this did not occur to the editor), as a real event which had really happened, instead of a portion of the Church service. I can only repeat, assuming as I am that it was a real event and did actually happen, that it was as complete a success as any in history. Christianity as a specific doctrine was slain with Jesus, suddenly and utterly. He was hardly cold in his grave, or high in his heaven (as you please), before the apostles dragged the tradition of him down to the level of the thing it has remained ever since. And that thing the intelligent heathen may study, if they would be instructed in it by modern books, in Samuel Butler's novel, The Way of All Flesh.

THE VINDICTIVE MIRACLES AND THE STONING OF STEPHEN.

Take, for example, the miracles. Of Jesus alone of all the Christian miracle workers there is no record, except in certain gospels that all men reject, of a malicious or destructive miracle. A barren fig-tree was the only victim of his anger. Every one of his miracles on sentient subjects was an act of kindness. John declares that he healed the wound of the man whose ear was cut off (by Peter, John says) at the arrest in the garden. One of the first things the apostles did with their miraculous power was to strike dead a wretched man and his wife who had defrauded them by holding back some money from the common stock. They struck people blind or dead without remorse, judging because they had been judged. They healed the sick and raised the dead apparently in a spirit of pure display and advertisement. Their doctrine did not contain a ray of that light which reveals Jesus as one of the redeemers of men from folly and error. They cancelled him, and went back straight to John the Baptist and his formula of securing remission of sins by repentance and the rite of baptism (being born again of water and the spirit). Peter's first harangue softens us by the human touch of its exordium, which was a quaint assurance to his hearers that they must believe him to be sober because it was too early in the day to get drunk; but of Jesus he had nothing to say except that he was the Christ foretold by the prophets as coming from the seed of David, and that they must believe this and be baptized. To this the other apostles added incessant denunciations of the Jews for having crucified him, and threats of the destruction that would overtake them if they did not repent: that is, if they did not join the sect which the apostles were now forming. A quite intolerable young speaker named Stephen delivered an oration to the council, in which he first inflicted on them a tedious sketch of the history of Israel, with which they were presumably as well acquainted as he, and then reviled them in the most insulting terms as "stiffnecked and uncircumcized." Finally, after boring and annoying them to the utmost bearable extremity, he looked up and declared that he saw the heavens open, and Christ standing on the right hand of God. This was too much: they threw him out of the city and stoned him to death. It was a severe way of suppressing a tactless and conceited bore; but it was pardonable and human in comparison to the slaughter of poor Ananias and Sapphira.

PAUL.

Suddenly a man of genius, Paul, violently anti-Christian, enters on the scene, holding the clothes of the men who are stoning Stephen. He persecutes the Christians with great vigor, a sport which he combines with the business of a tentmaker. This temperamental hatred of Jesus, whom he has never seen, is a pathological symptom of that particular sort of conscience and nervous constitution which brings its victims under the tyranny of two delirious terrors: the terror of sin and the terror of death, which may be called also the terror of sex and the terror of life. Now Jesus, with his healthy conscience on his higher plane, was free from these terrors. He consorted freely with sinners, and was never concerned for a moment, as far as we know, about whether his conduct was sinful or not; so that he has forced us to accept him as the man without sin. Even if we reckon his last days as the days of his delusion, he none the less gave a fairly convincing exhibition of superiority to the fear of death. This must have both fascinated and horrified Paul, or Saul, as he was first called. The horror accounts for his fierce persecution of the Christians. The fascination accounts for the strangest of his fancies: the fancy for attaching the name of Jesus Christ to the great idea which flashed upon him on the road to Damascus, the idea that he could not only make a religion of his two terrors, but that the movement started by Jesus offered him the nucleus for his new Church. It was a monstrous idea; and the shocks of it, as he afterwards declared, struck him blind for days. He heard Jesus calling to him from the clouds, "Why persecute me?" His natural hatred of the teacher for whom Sin and Death had no terrors turned into a wild personal worship of him which has the ghastliness of a beautiful thing seen in a false light.

The chronicler of the Acts of the Apostles sees nothing of the significance of this. The great danger of conversion in all ages has been that when the religion of the high mind is offered to the lower mind, the lower mind, feeling its fascination without understanding it, and being incapable of rising to it, drags it down to its level by degrading it. Years ago I said that the conversion of a savage to Christianity is the conversion of Christianity to savagery. The conversion of Paul was no conversion at all: it was Paul who converted the religion that had raised one man above sin and death into a religion that delivered millions of men so completely into their dominion that their own common nature became a horror to them, and the religious life became a denial of life. Paul had no intention of surrendering either his Judaism or his Roman citizenship to the new moral world (as Robert Owen called it) of Communism and Jesuism. Just as in the XIX century Karl Marx, not content to take political economy as he found it, insisted on rebuilding it from the bottom upwards in his own way, and thereby gave a new lease of life to the errors it was just outgrowing, so Paul reconstructed the old Salvationism from which Jesus had vainly tried to redeem him, and produced a fantastic theology which is still the most amazing thing of the kind known to us. Being intellectually an inveterate Roman Rationalist, always discarding the irrational real thing for the unreal but ratiocinable postulate, he began by discarding Man as he is, and substituted a postulate which he called Adam. And when he was asked, as he surely must have been in a world not wholly mad, what had become of the natural man, he replied "Adam IS the natural man." This was confusing to simpletons, because according to tradition Adam was certainly the name of the natural man as created in the garden of Eden. It was as if a preacher of our own time had described as typically British Frankenstein's monster, and called him Smith, and somebody, on demanding what about the man in the street, had been told "Smith is the man in the street." The thing happens often enough; for indeed the world is full of these Adams and Smiths and men in the street and average sensual men and economic men and womanly women and what not, all of them imaginary Atlases carrying imaginary worlds on their unsubstantial shoulders.

The Eden story provided Adam with a sin: the "original sin" for which we are all damned. Baldly stated, this seems ridiculous; nevertheless it corresponds to something actually existent not only in Paul's consciousness but in our own. The original sin was not the eating of the forbidden fruit, but the consciousness of sin which the fruit produced. The moment Adam and Eve tasted the apple they found themselves ashamed of their sexual relation, which until then had seemed quite innocent to them; and there is no getting over the hard fact that this shame, or state of sin, has persisted to this day, and is one of the strongest of our instincts. Thus Paul's postulate of Adam as the natural man was pragmatically true: it worked. But the weakness of Pragmatism is that most theories will work if you put your back into making them work, provided they have some point of contact with human nature. Hedonism will pass the pragmatic test as well as Stoicism. Up to a certain point every social principle that is not absolutely idiotic works: Autocracy works in Russia and Democracy in America; Atheism works in France, Polytheism in India, Monotheism throughout Islam, and Pragmatism, or No-ism, in England. Paul's fantastic conception of the damned Adam, represented by Bunyan as a pilgrim with a great burden of sins on his back, corresponded to the fundamental condition of evolution, which is, that life, including human life, is continually evolving, and must therefore be continually ashamed of itself and its present and past. Bunyan's pilgrim wants to get rid of his bundle of sins; but he also wants to reach "yonder shining light;" and when at last his bundle falls off him into the sepulchre of Christ, his pilgrimage is still unfinished and his hardest trials still ahead of him. His conscience remains uneasy; "original sin" still torments him; and his adventure with Giant Despair, who throws him into the dungeon of Doubting Castle, from which he escapes by the use of a skeleton key, is more terrible than any he met whilst the bundle was still on his back. Thus Bunyan's allegory of human nature breaks through the Pauline theology at a hundred points. His theological allegory, The Holy War, with its troops of Election Doubters, and its cavalry of "those that rode Reformadoes," is, as a whole, absurd, impossible, and, except in passages where the artistic old Adam momentarily got the better of the Salvationist theologian, hardly readable.

Paul's theory of original sin was to some extent idiosyncratic. He tells us definitely that he finds himself quite well able to avoid the sinfulness of sex by practising celibacy; but he recognizes, rather contemptuously, that in this respect he is not as other men are, and says that they had better marry than burn, thus admitting that though marriage may lead to placing the desire to please wife or husband before the desire to please God, yet preoccupation with unsatisfied desire may be even more ungodly than preoccupation with domestic affection. This view of the case inevitably led him to insist that a wife should be rather a slave than a partner, her real function being, not to engage a man's love and loyalty, but on the contrary to release them for God by relieving the man of all preoccupation with sex just as in her capacity of a housekeeper and cook she relieves his preoccupation with hunger by the simple expedient of satisfying his appetite. This slavery also justifies itself pragmatically by working effectively; but it has made Paul the eternal enemy of Woman. Incidentally it has led to many foolish surmises about Paul's personal character and circumstance, by people so enslaved by sex that a celibate appears to them a sort of monster. They forget that not only whole priesthoods, official and unofficial, from Paul to Carlyle and Ruskin, have defied the tyranny of sex, but immense numbers of ordinary citizens of both sexes have, either voluntarily or under pressure of circumstances easily surmountable, saved their energies for less primitive activities.

Howbeit, Paul succeeded in stealing the image of Christ crucified for the figure-head of his Salvationist vessel, with its Adam posing as the natural man, its doctrine of original sin, and its damnation avoidable only by faith in the sacrifice of the cross. In fact, no sooner had Jesus knocked over the dragon of superstition than Paul boldly set it on its legs again in the name of Jesus.

THE CONFUSION OF CHRISTENDOM.

Now it is evident that two religions having such contrary effects on mankind should not be confused as they are under a common name. There is not one word of Pauline Christianity in the characteristic utterances of Jesus. When Saul watched the clothes of the men who stoned Stephen, he was not acting upon beliefs which Paul renounced. There is no record of Christ's having ever said to any man: "Go and sin as much as you like: you can put it all on me." He said "Sin no more," and insisted that he was putting up the standard of conduct, not debasing it, and that the righteousness of the Christian must exceed that of the Scribe and Pharisee. The notion that he was shedding his blood in order that every petty cheat and adulterator and libertine might wallow in it and come out whiter than snow, cannot be imputed to him on his own authority. "I come as an infallible patent medicine for bad consciences" is not one of the sayings in the gospels. If Jesus could have been consulted on Bunyan's allegory as to that business of the burden of sin dropping from the pilgrim's back when he caught sight of the cross, we must infer from his teaching that he would have told Bunyan in forcible terms that he had never made a greater mistake in his life, and that the business of a Christ was to make self-satisfied sinners feel the burden of their sins and stop committing them instead of assuring them that they could not help it, as it was all Adam's fault, but that it did not matter as long as they were credulous and friendly about himself. Even when he believed himself to be a god, he did not regard himself as a scapegoat. He was to take away the sins of the world by good government, by justice and mercy, by setting the welfare of little children above the pride of princes, by casting all the quackeries and idolatries which now usurp and malversate the power of God into what our local authorities quaintly call the dust destructor, and by riding on the clouds of heaven in glory instead of in a thousand-guinea motor car. That was delirious, if you like; but it was the delirium of a free soul, not of a shamebound one like Paul's. There has really never been a more monstrous imposition perpetrated than the imposition of the limitations of Paul's soul upon the soul of Jesus.

THE SECRET OF PAUL'S SUCCESS.

Paul must soon have found that his followers had gained peace of mind and victory over death and sin at the cost of all moral responsibility; for he did his best to reintroduce it by making good conduct the test of sincere belief, and insisting that sincere belief was necessary to salvation. But as his system was rooted in the plain fact that as what he called sin includes sex and is therefore an ineradicable part of human nature (why else should Christ have had to atone for the sin of all future generations?) it was impossible for him to declare that sin, even in its wickedest extremity, could forfeit the sinner's salvation if he repented and believed. And to this day Pauline Christianity is, and owes its enormous vogue to being, a premium on sin. Its consequences have had to be held in check by the worldlywise majority through a violently anti-Christian system of criminal law and stern morality. But of course the main restraint is human nature, which has good impulses as well as bad ones, and refrains from theft and murder and cruelty, even when it is taught that it can commit them all at the expense of Christ and go happily to heaven afterwards, simply because it does not always want to murder or rob or torture.

It is now easy to understand why the Christianity of Jesus failed completely to establish itself politically and socially, and was easily suppressed by the police and the Church, whilst Paulinism overran the whole western civilized world, which was at that time the Roman Empire, and was adopted by it as its official faith, the old avenging gods falling helplessly before the new Redeemer. It still retains, as we may see in Africa, its power of bringing to simple people a message of hope and consolation that no other religion offers. But this enchantment is produced by its spurious association with the personal charm of Jesus, and exists only for untrained minds. In the hands of a logical Frenchman like Calvin, pushing it to its utmost conclusions, and devising "institutes" for hardheaded adult Scots and literal Swiss, it becomes the most infernal of fatalisms; and the lives of civilized children are blighted by its logic whilst negro piccaninnies are rejoicing in its legends.

PAUL'S QUALITIES

Paul, however, did not get his great reputation by mere imposition and reaction. It is only in comparison with Jesus (to whom many prefer him) that he appears common and conceited. Though in The Acts he is only a vulgar revivalist, he comes out in his own epistles as a genuine poet,--though by flashes only. He is no more a Christian than Jesus was a Baptist; he is a disciple of Jesus only as Jesus was a disciple of John. He does nothing that Jesus would have done, and says nothing that Jesus would have said, though much, like the famous ode to charity, that he would have admired. He is more Jewish than the Jews, more Roman than the Romans, proud both ways, full of startling confessions and self-revelations that would not surprise us if they were slipped into the pages of Nietzsche, tormented by an intellectual conscience that demanded an argued case even at the cost of sophistry, with all sorts of fine qualities and occasional illuminations, but always hopelessly in the toils of Sin, Death, and Logic, which had no power over Jesus. As we have seen, it was by introducing this bondage and terror of his into the Christian doctrine that he adapted it to the Church and State systems which Jesus transcended, and made it practicable by destroying the specifically Jesuist side of it. He would have been quite in his place in any modern Protestant State; and he, not Jesus, is the true head and founder of our Reformed Church, as Peter is of the Roman Church. The followers of Paul and Peter made Christendom, whilst the Nazarenes were wiped out.

THE ACTS OF THE APOSTLES.

Here we may return to the narrative called The Acts of the Apostles, which we left at the point where the stoning of Stephen was followed by the introduction of Paul. The author of The Acts, though a good story-teller, like Luke, was (herein also like Luke) much weaker in power of thought than in imaginative literary art. Hence we find Luke credited with the authorship of The Acts by people who like stories and have no aptitude for theology, whilst the book itself is denounced as spurious by Pauline theologians because Paul, and indeed all the apostles, are represented in it as very commonplace revivalists, interesting us by their adventures more than by any qualities of mind or character. Indeed, but for the epistles, we should have a very poor opinion of the apostles. Paul in particular is described as setting a fashion which has remained in continual use to this day. Whenever he addresses an audience, he dwells with great zest on his misdeeds before his pseudo conversion, with the effect of throwing into stronger relief his present state of blessedness; and he tells the story of that conversion over and over again, ending with exhortations to the hearers to come and be saved, and threats of the wrath that will overtake them if they refuse. At any revival meeting today the same thing may be heard, followed by the same conversions. This is natural enough; but it is totally unlike the preaching of Jesus, who never talked about his personal history, and never "worked up" an audience to hysteria. It aims at a purely nervous effect; it brings no enlightenment; the most ignorant man has only to become intoxicated with his own vanity, and mistake his self-satisfaction for the Holy Ghost, to become qualified as an apostle; and it has absolutely nothing to do with the characteristic doctrines of Jesus. The Holy Ghost may be at work all round producing wonders of art and science, and strengthening men to endure all sorts of martyrdoms for the enlargement of knowledge, and the enrichment and intensification of life ("that ye may have life more abundantly"); but the apostles, as described in The Acts, take no part in the struggle except as persecutors and revilers. To this day, when their successors get the up-per hand, as in Geneva (Knox's "perfect city of Christ") and in Scotland and Ulster, every spiritual activity but moneymaking and churchgoing is stamped out; heretics are ruthlessly persecuted; and such pleasures as money can purchase are suppressed so that its possessors are compelled to go on making money because there is nothing else to do. And the compensation for all this privation is partly an insane conceit of being the elect of God, with a reserved seat in heaven, and partly, since even the most infatuated idiot cannot spend his life admiring himself, the less innocent ex-citement of punishing other people for not admiring him, and the nosing out of the sins of the people who, being intelligent enough to be incapable of mere dull self-righteousness, and highly susceptible to the beauty and interest of the real workings of the Holy Ghost, try to live more rational and abundant lives. The abominable amusement of terrifying children with threats of hell is another of these diversions, and perhaps the vilest and most mischievous of them. The net result is that the imitators of the apostles, whether they are called Holy Willies or Stigginses in deri-sion, or, in admiration, Puritans or saints, are, outside their own congregations, and to a considerable extent inside them, heartily detested. Now nobody detests Jesus, though many who have been tormented in their childhood in his name include him in their general loathing of everything connected with the word religion; whilst others, who know him only by misrepresentation as a sentimental pacifist and an ascetic, include him in their general dislike of that type of character. In the same way a student who has had to "get up" Shakespear as a college subject may hate Shakespear; and people who dislike the theatre may include Moliere in that dislike without ever having read a line of his or witnessed one of his plays; but nobody with any knowledge of Shakespear or Moliere could possibly detest them, or read without pity and horror a description of their being insulted, tortured, and killed. And the same is true of Jesus. But it requires the most strenuous effort of conscience to refrain from crying "Serve him right" when we read of the stoning of Stephen; and nobody has ever cared twopence about the martyrdom of Peter: many better men have died worse deaths: for example, honest Hugh Latimer, who was burned by us, was worth fifty Stephens and a dozen Peters. One feels at last that when Jesus called Peter from his boat, he spoiled an honest fisherman, and made nothing better out of the wreck than a salvation monger.

THE CONTROVERSIES ON BAPTISM AND TRANSUBSTANTIATION.

Meanwhile the inevitable effect of dropping the peculiar doctrines of Jesus and going back to John the Baptist, was to make it much easier to convert Gentiles than Jews; and it was by following the line of least resistance that Paul became the apostle to the Gentiles. The Jews had their own rite of initiation: the rite of circumcision; and they were fiercely jealous for it, because it marked them as the chosen people of God, and set them apart from the Gentiles, who were simply the uncircumcized. When Paul, finding that baptism made way faster among the Gentiles than among the Jews, as it enabled them to plead that they too were sanctified by a rite of later and higher authority than the Mosaic rite, he was compelled to admit that circumcision did not matter; and this, to the Jews, was an intolerable blasphemy. To Gentiles like ourselves, a good deal of the Epistle to the Romans is now tedious to unreadableness because it consists of a hopeless attempt by Paul to evade the conclusion that if a man were baptized it did not matter a rap whether he was circumcized or not. Paul claims circumcision as an excellent thing in its way for a Jew; but if it has no efficacy towards salvation, and if salvation is the one thing needful--and Paul was committed to both propositions--his pleas in mitigation only made the Jews more determined to stone him.

Thus from the very beginning of apostolic Christianity, it was hampered by a dispute as to whether salvation was to be attained by a surgical operation or by a sprinkling of water: mere rites on which Jesus would not have wasted twenty words. Later on, when the new sect conquered the Gentile west, where the dispute had no practical application, the other ceremony--that of eating the god--produced a still more disastrous dispute, in which a difference of belief, not as to the obligation to perform the ceremony, but as to whether it was a symbolic or a real ingestion of divine substance, produced persecution, slaughter, hatred, and everything that Jesus loathed, on a monstrous scale.

But long before that, the superstitions which had fastened on the new faith made trouble. The parthenogenetic birth of Christ, simple enough at first as a popular miracle, was not left so simple by the theologians. They began to ask of what substance Christ was made in the womb of the virgin. When the Trinity was added to the faith the question arose, was the virgin the mother of God or only the mother of Jesus? Arian schisms and Nestorian schisms arose on these questions; and the leaders of the resultant agitations rancorously deposed one another and excommunicated one another according to their luck in enlisting the emperors on their side. In the IV century they began to burn one another for differences of opinion in such matters. In the VIII century Charlemagne made Christianity compulsory by killing those who refused to embrace it; and though this made an end of the voluntary character of conversion, Charlemagne may claim to be the first Christian who put men to death for any point of doctrine that really mattered. From his time onward the history of Christian controversy reeks with blood and fire, torture and warfare. The Crusades, the persecutions in Albi and elsewhere, the Inquisition, the "wars of religion" which followed the Reformation, all presented themselves as Christian phenomena; but who can doubt that they would have been repudiated with horror by Jesus? Our own notion that the massacre of St. Bartholomew's was an outrage on Christianity, whilst the campaigns of Gustavus Adolphus, and even of Frederick the Great, were a defence of it, is as absurd as the opposite notion that Frederick was Antichrist and Torquemada and Ignatius Loyola men after the very heart of Jesus. Neither they nor their exploits had anything to do with him. It is probable that Archbishop Laud and John Wesley died equally persuaded that he in whose name they had made themselves famous on earth would receive them in Heaven with open arms. Poor Fox the Quaker would have had ten times their chance; and yet Fox made rather a miserable business of life.

Nevertheless all these perversions of the doctrine of Jesus derived their moral force from his credit, and so had to keep his gospel alive. When the Protestants translated the Bible into the vernacular and let it loose among the people, they did an extremely dangerous thing, as the mischief which followed proves; but they incidentally let loose the sayings of Jesus in open competition with the sayings of Paul and Koheleth and David and Solomon and the authors of Job and the Pentateuch; and, as we have seen, Jesus seems to be the winning name. The glaring contradiction between his teaching and the practice of all the States and all the Churches is no longer hidden. And it may be that though nineteen centuries have passed since

Jesus was born (the date of his birth is now quaintly given as 7 B.C., though some contend for 100 B.C.), and though his Church has not yet been founded nor his political system tried, the bankruptcy of all the other systems when audited by our vital statistics, which give us a final test for all political systems, is driving us hard into accepting him, not as a scapegoat, but as one who was much less of a fool in practical matters than we have hitherto all thought him.

THE ALTERNATIVE CHRISTS.

Let us now clear up the situation a little. The New Testament tells two stories for two different sorts of readers. One is the old story of the achievement of our salvation by the sacrifice and atonement of a divine personage who was barbarously slain and rose again on the third day: the story as it was accepted by the apostles. And in this story the political, economic, and moral views of the Christ have no importance: the atonement is everything; and we are saved by our faith in it, and not by works or opinions (other than that particular opinion) bearing on practical affairs.

The other is the story of a prophet who, after expressing several very interesting opinions as to practical conduct, both personal and political, which are now of pressing importance, and instructing his disciples to carry them out in their daily life, lost his head; believed himself to be a crude legendary form of god; and under that delusion courted and suffered a cruel execution in the belief that he would rise from the dead and come in glory to reign over a regenerated world. In this form, the political, economic and moral opinions of Jesus, as guides to conduct, are interesting and important: the rest is mere psychopathy and superstition. The accounts of the resurrection, the parthenogenetic birth, and the more incredible miracles are rejected as inventions; and such episodes as the conversation with the devil are classed with similar conversations recorded of St. Dunstan, Luther, Bunyan, Swedenborg, and Blake.

CREDULITY NO CRITERION.

This arbitrary acceptance and rejection of parts of the gospel is not peculiar to the Secularist view. We have seen Luke and John reject Matthew's story of the massacre of the innocents and the flight into Egypt without ceremony. The notion that Matthew's manuscript is a literal and infallible record of facts, not subject to the errors that beset all earthly chroniclers, would have made John stare, being as it is a comparatively modern fancy of intellectually untrained people who keep the Bible on the same shelf, with Napoleon's Book of Fate, Old Moore's Almanack, and handbooks of therapeutic herbalism. You may be a fanatical Salvationist and reject more miracle stories than Huxley did; and you may utterly repudiate Jesus as the Savior and yet cite him as a historical witness to the possession by men of the most marvellous thaumaturgical powers. "Christ Scientist" and Jesus the Mahatma are preached by people whom Peter would have struck dead as worse infidels than Simon Magus; and the Atonement; is preached by Baptist and Congregationalist ministers whose views of the miracles are those of Ingersoll and Bradlaugh. Luther, who made a clean sweep of all the saints with their million miracles, and reduced the Blessed Virgin herself to the status of an idol, concentrated Salvationism to a point at which the most execrable murderer who believes in it when the rope is round his neck, flies straight to the arms of Jesus, whilst Tom Paine and Shelley fall into the bottomless pit to burn there to all eternity. And sceptical physicists like Sir William Crookes demonstrate by laboratory experiments that "mediums" like Douglas Home can make the pointer of a spring-balance go round without touching the weight suspended from it.

BELIEF IN PERSONAL IMMORTALITY
NO CRITERION.

Nor is belief in individual immortality any criterion. Theosophists, rejecting vicarious atonement so sternly that they insist that the smallest of our sins brings its Karma, also insist on individual immortality and metempsychosis in order to provide an unlimited field for Karma to be worked out by the unredeemed sinner. The belief in the prolongation of individual life beyond the grave is far more real and vivid among table-rapping Spiritualists than among conventional Christians. The notion that those who reject the Christian (or any other) scheme of salvation by atonement must reject also belief in personal immortality and in miracles is as baseless as the notion that if a man is an atheist he will steal your watch.

I could multiply these instances to weariness. The main difference that set Gladstone and Huxley by the ears is not one between belief in supernatural persons or miraculous events and the sternest view of such belief as a breach of intellectual integrity: it is the difference between belief in the efficacy of the crucifixion as an infallible cure for guilt, and a congenital incapacity for believing this, or (the same thing) desiring to believe it.

THE SECULAR VIEW NATURAL, NOT RATIONAL, THEREFORE INEVITABLE.

It must therefore be taken as a flat fundamental modern fact, whether we like it or not, that whilst many of us cannot believe that Jesus got his curious grip of our souls by mere sentimentality, neither can we believe that he was John Barleycorn. The more our reason and study lead us to believe that Jesus was talking the most penetrating good sense when he preached Communism; when he declared that the reality behind the popular belief in God was a creative spirit in ourselves, called by him the Heavenly Father and by us Evolution, Elan Vital, Life Force and other names; when he protested against the claims of marriage and the family to appropriate that high part of our energy that was meant for the service of his Father, the more impossible it becomes for us to believe that he was talking equally good sense when he so suddenly announced that he was himself a visible concrete God; that his flesh and blood were miraculous food for us; that he must be tortured and slain in the traditional manner and would rise from the dead after three days; and that at his second coming the stars would fall from heaven and he become king of an earthly paradise. But it is easy and reasonable to believe that an overwrought preacher at last went mad as Swift and Ruskin and Nietzsche went mad. Every asylum has in it a patient suffering from the delusion that he is a god, yet otherwise sane enough. These patients do not nowadays declare that they will be barbarously slain and will rise from the dead, because they have lost that tradition of the destiny of godhead; but they claim everything appertaining to divinity that is within their knowledge.

Thus the gospels as memoirs and suggestive statements of sociological and biological doctrine, highly relevant to modern civilization, though ending in the history of a psycopathic delusion, are quite credible, intelligible, and interesting to modern thinkers. In any other light they are neither credible, intelligible, nor interesting except to people upon whom the delusion imposes.

"THE HIGHER CRITICISM."

Historical research and paleographic criticism will no doubt continue their demonstrations that the New Testament, like the Old, seldom tells a single story or expounds a single doctrine, and gives us often an accretion and conglomeration of widely discrete and even unrelated traditions and doctrines. But these disintegrations, though technically interesting to scholars, and gratifying or exasperating, as the case may be, to people who are merely defending or attacking the paper fortifications of the infallibility of the Bible, have hardly anything to do with the purpose of these pages. I have mentioned the fact that most of the authorities are now agreed (for the moment) that the date of the birth of Jesus may be placed at about 7 B.C.; but they do not therefore date their letters 1923, nor, I presume, do they expect me to do so. What I am engaged in is a criticism (in the Kantian sense) of an established body of belief which has become an actual part of the mental fabric of my readers; and I should be the most exasperating of triflers and pedants if I were to digress into a criticism of some other belief or no-belief which my readers might conceivably profess if they were erudite Scriptural paleographers and historians, in which case, by the way, they would have to change their views so frequently that the gospel they received in their childhood would dominate them after all by its superior persistency. The chaos of mere facts in which the Sermon on the Mount and the Ode to Charity suggest nothing but disputes as to whether they are interpolations or not, in which Jesus becomes nothing but a name suspected of belonging to ten different prophets or executed persons, in which Paul is only the man who could not possibly have written the epistles attributed to him, in which Chinese sages, Greek philosophers, Latin authors, and writers of ancient anonymous inscriptions are thrown at our heads as the sources of this or that scrap of the Bible, is neither a religion nor a criticism of religion: one does not offer the fact that a good deal of the medieval building in Peterborough Cathedral was found to be flagrant jerry-building as a criticism of the Dean's sermons. For good or evil, we have made a synthesis out of the literature we call the Bible; and though the discovery that there is a good deal of jerry-building in the Bible is interesting in its way, because everything about the Bible is interesting, it does not alter the synthesis very materially even for the paleographers, and does not alter it at all for those who know no more about modern paleography than Archbishop Ussher did. I have therefore indicated little more of the discoveries than Archbishop Ussher might have guessed for himself if he had read the Bible without prepossessions.

For the rest, I have taken the synthesis as it really lives and works in men. After all, a synthesis is what you want: it is the case you have to judge brought to an apprehensible issue for you. Even if you have little more respect for synthetic biography than for synthetic rubber, synthetic milk, and the still unachieved synthetic protoplasm which is to enable us to make different sorts of men as a pastry cook makes different sorts of tarts, the practical issue still lies as plainly before you as before the most credulous votaries of what pontificates as the Higher Criticism.

THE PERILS OF SALVATIONISM.

The secular view of Jesus is powerfully reinforced by the increase in our day of the number of people who have had the means of educating and training themselves to the point at which they are not afraid to look facts in the face, even such terrifying facts as sin and death. The result is greater sternness in modern thought. The conviction is spreading that to encourage a man to believe that though his sins be as scarlet he can be made whiter than snow by an easy exercise of self-conceit, is to encourage him to be a rascal. It did not work so badly when you could also conscientiously assure him that if he let himself be caught napping in the matter of faith by death, a red-hot hell would roast him alive to all eternity. In those days a sudden death--the most enviable of all deaths--was regarded as the most frightful calamity. It was classed with plague, pestilence, and famine, battle and murder, in our prayers. But belief in that hell is fast vanishing. All the leaders of thought have lost it; and even for the rank and file it has fled to those parts of Ireland and Scotland which are still in the XVII century. Even there, it is tacitly reserved for the other fellow.

THE IMPORTANCE OF HELL IN THE SALVATION SCHEME.

The seriousness of throwing over hell whilst still clinging to the Atonement is obvious. If there is no punishment for sin there can be no self-forgiveness for it. If Christ paid our score, and if there is no hell and therefore no chance of our getting into trouble by forgetting the obligation, then we can be as wicked as we like with impunity inside the secular law, even from self-reproach, which becomes mere ingratitude to the Savior. On the other hand, if Christ did not pay our score, it still stands against us; and such debts make us extremely uncomfortable. The drive of evolution, which we call conscience and honor, seizes on such slips, and shames us to the dust for being so low in the scale as to be capable of them. The "saved" thief experiences an ecstatic happiness which can never come to the honest atheist: he is tempted to steal again to repeat the glorious sensation. But if the atheist steals he has no such happiness. He is a thief and knows that he is a thief. Nothing can rub that off him. He may try to sooth his shame by some sort of restitution or equivalent act of benevolence; but that does not alter the fact that he did steal; and his conscience will not be easy until he has conquered his will to steal and changed himself into an honest man by developing that divine spark within him which Jesus insisted on as the everyday reality of what the atheist denies.

Now though the state of the believers in the atonement may thus be the happier, it is most certainly not more desirable from the point of view of the community. The fact that a believer is happier than a sceptic is no more to the point than the fact that a drunken man is happier than a sober one. The happiness of credulity is a cheap and dangerous quality of happiness, and by no means a necessity of life. Whether Socrates got as much happiness out of life as Wesley is an unanswerable question; but a nation of Socrateses would be much safer and happier than a nation of Wesleys; and its individuals would be higher in the evolutionary scale. At all events it is in the Socratic man and not in the Wesleyan that our hope lies now.

THE RIGHT TO REFUSE ATONEMENT.

Consequently, even if it were mentally possible for all of us to believe in the Atonement, we should have to cry off it, as we evidently have a right to do. Every man to whom salvation is offered has an inalienable natural right to say "No, thank you: I prefer to retain my full moral responsibility: it is not good for me to be able to load a scapegoat with my sins: I should be less careful how I committed them if I knew they would cost me nothing." Then, too, there is the attitude of Ibsen: that iron moralist to whom the whole scheme of salvation was only an ignoble attempt to cheat God; to get into heaven without paying the price. To be let off, to beg for and accept eternal life as a present instead of earning it, would be mean enough even if we accepted the contempt of the Power on whose pity we were trading; but to bargain for a crown of glory as well! that was too much for Ibsen: it provoked him to exclaim, "Your God is an old man whom you cheat," and to lash the deadened conscience of the XIX century back to life with a whip of scorpions.

THE TEACHING OF CHRISTIANITY.

And there I must leave the matter to such choice as your nature allows you. The honest teacher who has to make known to a novice the facts about Christianity cannot in any essential regard, I think, put the facts otherwise than as I have put them. If children are to be delivered from the proselytizing atheist on the one hand, and the proselytizing nun in the convent school on the other, with all the other proselytizers that lie between them, they must not be burdened with idle contro-versies as to whether there was ever such a person as Jesus or not. When Hume said that Joshua's campaigns were impossible, Whately did not wrangle about it: he proved, on the same lines, that the campaigns of Napoleon were impossible. Only fictitious characters will stand Hume's sort of examination: nothing will ever make Edward the Confessor and St. Louis as real to us as Don Quixote and Mr. Pickwick. We must cut the controversy short by declaring that there is the same evidence for the existence of Jesus as for that of any other person of his time; and the fact that you may not believe everything Matthew tells you no more disproves the existence of Jesus than the fact that you do not believe everything Macaulay tells you dis-proves the existence of William III. The gospel narratives in the main give you a biography which is quite credible and accountable on purely secular grounds when you have trimmed off everything that Hume or Grimm or Rousseau or Huxley or any modern bishop could reject as fanciful. Without going further than this, you can become a follower of Jesus just as you can become a follower of Confucius or Lao Tse, and may therefore call yourself a Jesuist, or even a Christian, if you hold, as the strictest Secularist quite legitimately may, that all prophets are inspired, and all men with a mission, Christs.

The teacher of Christianity has then to make known to the child, first the song of John Barleycorn, with the fields and seasons as witness to its eternal truth. Then, as the child's mind matures, it can learn, as historical and psychological phenom-ena, the tradition of the scapegoat, the Redeemer, the Atonement, the Resurrec-tion, the Second Coming, and how, in a world saturated with this tradition, Jesus has been largely accepted as the long expected and often prophesied Redeemer, the Messiah, the Christ. It is open to the child also to accept him. If the child is built like Gladstone, he will accept Jesus as his Savior, and Peter and John the Baptist as the Savior's revealer and forerunner respectively. If he is built like Huxley, he will take the secular view, in spite of all that a pious family can do to prevent him. The important thing now is that the Gladstones and Huxleys should no longer waste their time irrelevantly and ridiculously wrangling about the Gadarene swine, and that they should make up their minds as to the soundness of the secular doctrines of Jesus; for it is about these that they may come to blows in our own time.

CHRISTIANITY AND THE EMPIRE.

Finally, let us ask why it is that the old superstitions have so suddenly lost countenance that although, to the utter disgrace of the nation's leaders and rulers, the laws by which persecutors can destroy or gag all freedom of thought and speech in these matters are still unrepealed and ready to the hand of our bigots and fanatics (quite recently a respectable shopkeeper was convicted of "blasphemy" for saying that if a modern girl accounted for an illicit pregnancy by saying she had conceived of the Holy Ghost, we should know what to think: a remark which would never have occurred to him had he been properly taught how the story was grafted on the gospel), yet somehow they are used only against poor men, and that only in a half-hearted way. When we consider that from the time when the first scholar ventured to whisper as a professional secret that the Pentateuch could not possibly have been written by Moses to the time within my own recollection when Bishop Colenso, for saying the same thing openly, was inhibited from preaching and actually excommunicated, eight centuries elapsed (the point at issue, though technically interesting to paleographers and historians, having no more bearing on human welfare than the controversy as to whether uncial or cursive is the older form of writing); yet now, within fifty years of Colenso's heresy, there is not a Churchman of any authority living, or an educated layman, who could without ridicule declare that Moses wrote the Pentateuch as Pascal wrote his Thoughts or D'Aubigny his History of the Reformation, or that St. Jerome wrote the passage about the three witnesses in the Vulgate, or that there are less than three different accounts of the creation jumbled together in the book of Genesis. Now the maddest Progressive will hardly contend that our growth in wisdom and liberality has been greater in the last half century than in the sixteen half centuries preceding: indeed it would be easier to sustain the thesis that the last fifty years have witnessed a distinct reaction from Victorian Liberalism to Collectivism which has perceptibly strengthened the State Churches. Yet the fact remains that whereas Byron's Cain, published a century ago, is a leading case on the point that there is no copyright in a blasphemous book, the Salvation Army might now include it among its publications without shocking anyone.

I suggest that the causes which have produced this sudden clearing of the air include the transformation of many modern States, notably the old self-contained French Republic and the tight little Island of Britain, into empires which overflow the frontiers of all the Churches. In India, for example, there are less than four million Christians out of a population of three hundred and sixteen and a half millions. The King of England is the defender of the faith; but what faith is now THE faith? The inhabitants of this island would, within the memory of persons still living, have claimed that their faith is surely the faith of God, and that all others are heathen. But we islanders are only forty-five millions; and if we count ourselves all as Christians, there are still seventy-seven and a quarter million Mahometans in the Empire. Add to these the Hindoos and Buddhists, Sikhs and Jains, whom I was taught in my childhood, by way of religious instruction, to regard as gross idolators consigned to eternal perdition, but whose faith I can now be punished for disparaging by a provocative word, and you have a total of over three hundred and forty-two and a quarter million heretics to swamp our forty-five million Britons, of whom, by the way, only six thousand call themselves distinctively "disciples of Christ," the rest being members of the Church of England and other denominations whose discipleship is less emphatically affirmed. In short, the Englishman of today, instead of being, like the forefathers whose ideas he clings to, a subject of a State practically wholly Christian, is now crowded, and indeed considerably overcrowded, into a corner of an Empire in which the Christians are a mere eleven per cent of the population; so that the Nonconformist who allows his umbrella stand to be sold up rather than pay rates towards the support of a Church of England school, finds himself paying taxes not only to endow the Church of Rome in Malta, but to send Christians to prison for the blasphemy of offering Bibles for sale in the streets of Khartoum. Turn to France, a country ten times more insular in its preoccupation with its own language, its own history, its own character, than we, who have always been explorers and colonizers and grumblers. This once self-centred nation is forty millions strong. The total population of the French Republic is about one hundred and fourteen millions. The French are not in our hopeless Christian minority of eleven per cent; but they are in a minority of thirty-five per cent, which is fairly conclusive. And, being a more logical people than we, they have officially abandoned Christianity and declared that the French State has no specific religion.

Neither has the British State, though it does not say so. No doubt there are many innocent people in England who take Charlemagne's view, and would, as a matter of course, offer our eighty-nine per cent of "pagans, I regret to say" the alternative of death or Christianity but for a vague impression that these lost ones are all being converted gradually by the missionaries. But no statesman can entertain such ludicrously parochial delusions. No English king or French president can possibly govern on the assumption that the theology of Peter and Paul, Luther and Calvin, has any objective validity, or that the Christ is more than the Buddha, or Jehovah more than Krishna, or Jesus more or less human than Mahomet or Zoroaster or Confucius. He is actually compelled, in so far as he makes laws against blasphemy at all, to treat all the religions, including Christianity, as blasphemous, when paraded before people who are not accustomed to them and do not want them. And even that is a concession to a mischievous intolerance which an empire should use its control of education to eradicate.

On the other hand, Governments cannot really divest themselves of religion, or even of dogma. When Jesus said that people should not only live but live more abundantly, he was dogmatizing; and many Pessimist sages, including Shakespear, whose hero begged his friend to refrain from suicide in the words "Absent thee from felicity awhile," would say dogmatizing very perniciously. Indeed many preachers and saints declare, some of them in the name of Jesus himself, that this world is a vale of tears, and that our lives had better be passed in sorrow and even in torment, as a preparation for a better life to come. Make these sad people comfortable; and they baffle you by putting on hair shirts. None the less, governments must proceed on dogmatic assumptions, whether they call them dogmas or not; and they must clearly be assumptions common enough to stamp those who reject them as eccentrics or lunatics. And the greater and more heterogeneous the population the commoner the assumptions must be. A Trappist monastery can be conducted on assumptions which would in twenty-fours hours provoke the village at its gates to insurrection. That is because the monastery selects its people; and if a Trappist does not like it he can leave it. But a subject of the British Empire or the French Republic is not selected; and if he does not like it he must lump it; for emigration is practicable only within narrow limits, and seldom provides an effective remedy, all civilizations being now much alike. To anyone capable of comprehending government at all it must be evident without argument that the set of fundamental assumptions drawn up in the thirty-nine articles or in the Westminster Confession are wildly impossible as political constitutions for modern empires. A personal profession of them by any person disposed to take such professions seriously would practically disqualify him for high imperial office. A Calvinist Viceroy of India and a Particular Baptist Secretary of State for Foreign Affairs would wreck the empire. The Stuarts wrecked even the tight little island which was the nucleus of the empire by their Scottish logic and theological dogma; and it may be sustained very plausibly that the alleged aptitude of the English for self-government, which is contradicted by every chapter of their history, is really only an incurable inaptitude for theology, and indeed for co-ordinated thought in any direction, which makes them equally impatient of systematic despotism and systematic good government: their history being that of a badly governed and accidentally free people (comparatively). Thus our success in colonizing, as far as it has not been produced by exterminating the natives, has been due to our indifference to the salvation of our subjects. Ireland is the exception which proves the rule; for Ireland, the standing instance of the in- ability of the English to colonize without extermination of natives, is also the one country under British rule in which the conquerors and colonizers proceeded on the assumption that their business was to establish Protestantism as well as to make money and thereby secure at least the lives of the unfortunate inhabitants out of whose labor it could be made. At this moment Ulster is refusing to accept fellow- citizenship with the other Irish provinces because the south believes in St. Peter and Bossuet, and the north in St. Paul and Calvin. Imagine the effect of trying to govern India or Egypt from Belfast or from the Vatican!

The position is perhaps graver for France than for England, because the sixty- five per cent of French subjects who are neither French nor Christian nor Modern- ist includes some thirty millions of negroes who are susceptible, and indeed highly susceptible, of conversion to those salvationist forms of pseudo-Christianity which have produced all the persecutions and religious wars of the last fifteen hundred years. When the late explorer Sir Henry Stanley told me of the emotional grip which Christianity had over the Baganda tribes, and read me their letters, which were exactly like medieval letters in their literal faith and everpresent piety, I said "Can these men handle a rifle?" To which Stanley replied with some scorn "Of course they can, as well as any white man." Now at this moment (1915) a vast European war is being waged, in which the French are using Senegalese soldiers. I ask the French Government, which, like our own Government, is deliberately leaving the religious instruction of these negroes in the hands of missions of Petrine Catholics and Pauline Calvinists, whether they have considered the possibility of a new series of crusades, by ardent African Salvationists, to rescue Paris from the grip of the modern scientific "infidel," and to raise the cry of "Back to the Apostles: back to Charlemagne!" We are more fortunate in that an overwhelming majority of our subjects are Hindoos, Mahometans and Buddhists: that is, they have, as a prophylactic against salvationist Christianity, highly civilized religions of their own. Mahometanism, which Napoleon at the end of his career classed as perhaps the best popular religion for modern political use, might in some respects have arisen as a reformed Christianity if Mahomet had had to deal with a population of seventeenth-century Christians instead of Arabs who worshipped stones. As it is, men do not reject Mahomet for Calvin; and to offer a Hindoo so crude a theology as ours in exchange for his own, or our Jewish canonical literature as an improvement on Hindoo scripture, is to offer old lamps for older ones in a market where the oldest lamps, like old furniture in England, are the most highly valued. Yet, I repeat, government is impossible without a religion: that is, without a body of common assumptions. The open mind never acts: when we have done our utmost to arrive at a reasonable conclusion, we still, when we can reason and investigate no more, must close our minds for the moment with a snap, and act dogmatically on our conclusions. The man who waits to make an entirely reasonable will dies intestate. A man so reasonable as to have an open mind about theft and murder, or about the need for food and reproduction, might just as well be a fool and a scoundrel for any use he could be as a legislator or a State official. The modern pseudo-democratic statesman, who says that he is only in power to carry out the will of the people, and moves only as the cat jumps, is clearly a political and intellectual brigand. The rule of the negative man who has no convictions means in practice the rule of the positive mob. Freedom of conscience as Cromwell used the phrase is an excellent thing; nevertheless if any man had proposed to give effect to freedom of conscience as to cannibalism in England, Cromwell would have laid him by the heels almost as promptly as he would have laid a Roman Catholic, though in Fiji at the same moment he would have supported heartily the freedom of conscience of a vegetarian who disparaged the sacred diet of Long Pig.

Here then come in the importance of the repudiation by Jesus of proselytism. His rule "Don't pull up the tares: sow the wheat: if you try to pull up the tares you will pull up the wheat with it" is the only possible rule for a statesman governing a modern empire, or a voter supporting such a statesman. There is nothing in the teaching of Jesus that cannot be assented to by a Brahman, a Mahometan, a Buddhist or a Jew, without any question of their conversion to Christianity. In some ways it is easier to reconcile a Mahometan to Jesus than a British parson, because the idea of a professional priest is unfamiliar and even monstrous to a Mahometan (the tourist who persists in asking who is the dean of St. Sophia puzzles beyond words the sacristan who lends him a huge pair of slippers); and Jesus never suggested that his disciples should separate themselves from the laity: he picked them up by the wayside, where any man or woman might follow him. For priests he had not a civil word; and they showed their sense of his hostility by getting him killed as soon as possible. He was, in short, a thoroughgoing anti-Clerical. And though, as we have seen, it is only by political means that his doctrine can be put into practice, he not only never suggested a sectarian theocracy as a form of Government, and would certainly have prophesied the downfall of the late President Kruger if he had survived to his time, but, when challenged, he refused to teach his disciples not to pay tribute to Caesar, admitting that Caesar, who presumably had the kingdom of heaven within him as much as any disciple, had his place in the scheme of things. Indeed the apostles made this an excuse for carrying subservience to the State to a pitch of idolatry that ended in the theory of the divine right of kings, and provoked men to cut kings' heads off to restore some sense of proportion in the matter. Jesus certainly did not consider the overthrow of the Roman empire or the substitution of a new ecclesiastical organization for the Jewish Church or for the priesthood of the Roman gods as part of his program. He said that God was better than Mammon; but he never said that Tweedledum was better than Tweedledee; and that is why it is now possible for British citizens and statesmen to follow Jesus, though they cannot possibly follow either Tweedledum or Tweedledee without bringing the empire down with a crash on their heads. And at that I must leave it.

LONDON, December 1915.

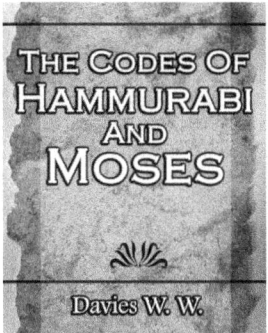

The Codes Of Hammurabi And Moses
W. W. Davies

QTY

The discovery of the Hammurabi Code is one of the greatest achievements of archaeology, and is of paramount interest, not only to the student of the Bible, but also to all those interested in ancient history...

Religion   **ISBN:** *1-59462-338-4*   **Pages:132**
MSRP $12.95

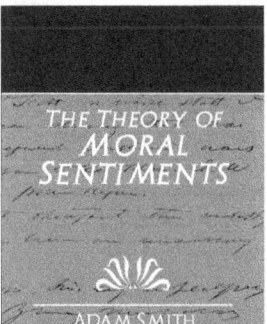

The Theory of Moral Sentiments
Adam Smith

QTY

This work from 1749. contains original theories of conscience amd moral judgment and it is the foundation for systemof morals.

Philosophy **ISBN:** *1-59462-777-0*   **Pages:536**
MSRP $19.95

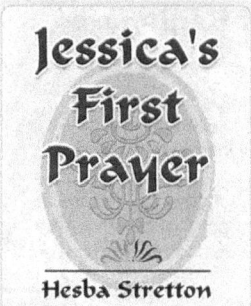

Jessica's First Prayer
Hesba Stretton

QTY

In a screened and secluded corner of one of the many railway-bridges which span the streets of London there could be seen a few years ago, from five o'clock every morning until half past eight, a tidily set-out coffee-stall, consisting of a trestle and board, upon which stood two large tin cans, with a small fire of charcoal burning under each so as to keep the coffee boiling during the early hours of the morning when the work-people were thronging into the city on their way to their daily toil...

Pages:84

Childrens   **ISBN:** *1-59462-373-2*   *MSRP $9.95*

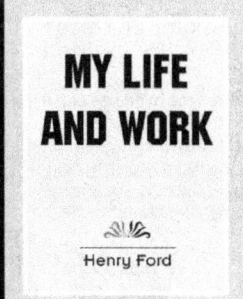

My Life and Work
Henry Ford

QTY

Henry Ford revolutionized the world with his implementation of mass production for the Model T automobile. Gain valuable business insight into his life and work with his own auto-biography... "We have only started on our development of our country we have not as yet, with all our talk of wonderful progress, done more than scratch the surface. The progress has been wonderful enough but..."

Pages:300

Biographies/   **ISBN:** *1-59462-198-5*   *MSRP $21.95*

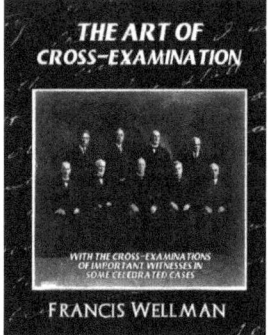

The Art of Cross-Examination
Francis Wellman

QTY

I presume it is the experience of every author, after his first book is published upon an important subject, to be almost overwhelmed with a wealth of ideas and illustrations which could readily have been included in his book, and which to his own mind, at least, seem to make a second edition inevitable. Such certainly was the case with me; and when the first edition had reached its sixth impression in five months, I rejoiced to learn that it seemed to my publishers that the book had met with a sufficiently favorable reception to justify a second and considerably enlarged edition. ..

Pages:412

Reference   ISBN: *1-59462-647-2*   *MSRP $19.95*

On the Duty of Civil Disobedience
Henry David Thoreau

QTY

Thoreau wrote his famous essay, On the Duty of Civil Disobedience, as a protest against an unjust but popular war and the immoral but popular institution of slave-owning. He did more than write—he declined to pay his taxes,   and was hauled off to gaol in consequence. Who can say how much this refusal of his hastened the end of the war and of slavery ?

Law   ISBN: *1-59462-747-9*   **Pages:48**

MSRP $7.45

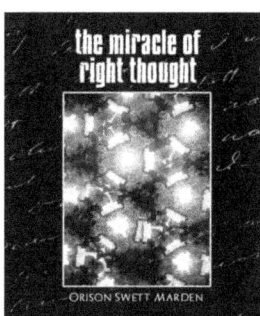

Dream Psychology
Psychoanalysis for Beginners

Sigmund Freud

Dream Psychology Psychoanalysis for Beginners
Sigmund Freud

QTY

Sigmund Freud, born Sigismund Schlomo Freud (May 6, 1856 - September 23, 1939), was a Jewish-Austrian neurologist and psychiatrist who co-founded the psychoanalytic school of psychology. Freud is best known for his theories of the unconscious mind, especially involving the mechanism of repression; his redefinition of sexual desire as mobile and directed towards a wide variety of objects; and his therapeutic techniques, especially his understanding of transference in the therapeutic relationship and the presumed value of dreams as sources of insight into unconscious desires.

Pages:196

Psychology   ISBN: *1-59462-905-6*   *MSRP $15.45*

The Miracle of Right Thought
Orison Swett Marden

QTY

Believe with all of your heart that you will do what you were made to do. When the mind has once formed the habit of holding cheerful, happy, prosperous pictures, it will not be easy to form the opposite habit. It does not matter how improbable or how far away this realization may see, or how dark the prospects may be, if we visualize them as best we can, as vividly as possible, hold tenaciously to them and vigorously struggle to attain them, they will gradually become actualized, realized in the life. But a desire, a longing without endeavor, a yearning abandoned or held indifferently will vanish without realization.

Pages:360

Self Help   ISBN: *1-59462-644-8*   *MSRP $25.45*

QTY

The Rosicrucian Cosmo-Conception Mystic Christianity *by Max Heindel*   ISBN: *1-59462-188-8*   **$38.95**
The Rosicrucian Cosmo-conception is not dogmatic, neither does it appeal to any other authority than the reason of the student. It is: not controversial, but is: sent forth in the, hope that it may help to clear...   *New Age/Religion Pages 646*

Abandonment To Divine Providence *by Jean-Pierre de Caussade*   ISBN: *1-59462-228-0*   **$25.95**
"The Rev. Jean Pierre de Caussade was one of the most remarkable spiritual writers of the Society of Jesus in France in the 18th Century. His death took place at Toulouse in 1751. His works have gone through many editions and have been republished...   *Inspirational/Religion Pages 400*

Mental Chemistry *by Charles Haanel*   ISBN: *1-59462-192-6*   **$23.95**
Mental Chemistry allows the change of material conditions by combining and appropriately utilizing the power of the mind. Much like applied chemistry creates something new and unique out of careful combinations of chemicals the mastery of mental chemistry...   *New Age Pages 354*

The Letters of Robert Browning and Elizabeth Barret Barrett 1845-1846 vol II   ISBN: *1-59462-193-4*   **$35.95**
by Robert Browning and Elizabeth Barrett   *Biographies Pages 596*

Gleanings In Genesis (volume I) *by Arthur W. Pink*   ISBN: *1-59462-130-6*   **$27.45**
Appropriately has Genesis been termed "the seed plot of the Bible" for in it we have, in germ form, almost all of the great doctrines which are afterwards fully developed in the books of Scripture which follow...   *Religion/Inspirational Pages 420*

The Master Key *by L. W. de Laurence*   ISBN: *1-59462-001-6*   **$30.95**
In no branch of human knowledge has there been a more lively increase of the spirit of research during the past few years than in the study of Psychology, Concentration and Mental Discipline. The requests for authentic lessons in Thought Control, Mental Discipline and...   *New Age/Business Pages 422*

The Lesser Key Of Solomon Goetia *by L. W. de Laurence*   ISBN: *1-59462-092-X*   **$9.95**
This translation of the first book of the "Lernegton" which is now for the first time made accessible to students of Talismanic Magic was done, after careful collation and edition, from numerous Ancient Manuscripts in Hebrew, Latin, and French...   *New Age/Occult Pages 92*

Rubaiyat Of Omar Khayyam *by Edward Fitzgerald*   ISBN:*1-59462-332-5*   **$13.95**
Edward Fitzgerald, whom the world has already learned, in spite of his own efforts to remain within the shadow of anonymity, to look upon as one of the rarest poets of the century, was born at Bredfield, in Suffolk, on the 31st of March, 1809. He was the third son of John Purcell...   *Music Pages 172*

Ancient Law *by Henry Maine*   ISBN: *1-59462-128-4*   **$29.95**
The chief object of the following pages is to indicate some of the earliest ideas of mankind, as they are reflected in Ancient Law, and to point out the relation of those ideas to modern thought.   *Religion/History Pages 452*

Far-Away Stories *by William J. Locke*   ISBN: *1-59462-129-2*   **$19.45**
"Good wine needs no bush, but a collection of mixed vintages does. And this book is just such a collection. Some of the stories I do not want to remain buried for ever in the museum files of dead magazine-numbers an author's not unpardonable vanity..."   *Fiction Pages 272*

Life of David Crockett *by David Crockett*   ISBN: *1-59462-250-7*   **$27.45**
"Colonel David Crockett was one of the most remarkable men of the times in which he lived. Born in humble life, but gifted with a strong will, an indomitable courage, and unremitting perseverance...   *Biographies/New Age Pages 424*

Lip-Reading *by Edward Nitchie*   ISBN: *1-59462-206-X*   **$25.95**
Edward B. Nitchie, founder of the New York School for the Hard of Hearing, now the Nitchie School of Lip-Reading, Inc, wrote "LIP-READING Principles and Practice". The development and perfecting of this meritorious work on lip-reading was an undertaking...   *How-to Pages 400*

A Handbook of Suggestive Therapeutics, Applied Hypnotism, Psychic Science   ISBN: *1-59462-214-0*   **$24.95**
by Henry Munro   *Health/New Age/Health/Self-help Pages 376*

A Doll's House: and Two Other Plays *by Henrik Ibsen*   ISBN: *1-59462-112-8*   **$19.95**
Henrik Ibsen created this classic when in revolutionary 1848 Rome. Introducing some striking concepts in playwriting for the realist genre, this play has been studied the world over.   *Fiction/Classics/Plays 308*

The Light of Asia *by sir Edwin Arnold*   ISBN: *1-59462-204-3*   **$13.95**
In this poetic masterpiece, Edwin Arnold describes the life and teachings of Buddha. The man who was to become known as Buddha to the world was born as Prince Gautama of India but he rejected the worldly riches and abandoned the reigns of power when... *Religion/History/Biographies Pages 170*

The Complete Works of Guy de Maupassant *by Guy de Maupassant*   ISBN: *1-59462-157-8*   **$16.95**
"For days and days, nights and nights, I had dreamed of that first kiss which was to consecrate our engagement, and I knew not on what spot I should put my lips..."   *Fiction/Classics Pages 240*

The Art of Cross-Examination *by Francis L. Wellman*   ISBN: *1-59462-309-0*   **$26.95**
Written by a renowned trial lawyer, Wellman imparts his experience and uses case studies to explain how to use psychology to extract desired information through questioning.   *How-to/Science/Reference Pages 408*

Answered or Unanswered? *by Louisa Vaughan*   ISBN: *1-59462-248-5*   **$10.95**
Miracles of Faith in China   *Religion Pages 112*

The Edinburgh Lectures on Mental Science (1909) *by Thomas*   ISBN: *1-59462-008-3*   **$11.95**
This book contains the substance of a course of lectures recently given by the writer in the Queen Street Hall, Edinburgh. Its purpose is to indicate the Natural Principles governing the relation between Mental Action and Material Conditions...   *New Age/Psychology Pages 148*

Ayesha *by H. Rider Haggard*   ISBN: *1-59462-301-5*   **$24.95**
Verily and indeed it is the unexpected that happens! Probably if there was one person upon the earth from whom the Editor of this, and of a certain previous history, did not expect to hear again...   *Classics Pages 380*

Ayala's Angel *by Anthony Trollope*   ISBN: *1-59462-352-X*   **$29.95**
The two girls were both pretty, but Lucy who was twenty-one who supposed to be simple and comparatively unattractive, whereas Ayala was credited, as her Bombwhat romantic name might show, with poetic charm and a taste for romance, Ayala when her father died was nineteen... *Fiction Pages 484*

The American Commonwealth *by James Bryce*   ISBN: *1-59462-286-8*   **$34.45**
An interpretation of American democratic political theory. It examines political mechanics and society from the perspective of Scotsman James Bryce   *Politics Pages 572*

Stories of the Pilgrims *by Margaret P. Pumphrey*   ISBN: *1-59462-116-2*   **$17.95**
This book explores pilgrims religious oppression in England as well as their escape to Holland and eventual crossing to America on the Mayflower, and their early days in New England...   *History Pages 268*

QTY

The Fasting Cure *by Sinclair Upton*   ISBN: *1-59462-222-1*   **$13.95**
*In the Cosmopolitan Magazine for May, 1910, and in the Contemporary Review (London) for April, 1910, I published an article dealing with my experi-
ences in fasting. I have written a great many magazine articles, but never one which attracted so much attention... New Age/Self Help/Health Pages 164*

Hebrew Astrology *by Sepharial*   ISBN: *1-59462-308-2*   **$13.45**
*In these days of advanced thinking it is a matter of common observation that we have left many of the old landmarks behind and that we are now pressing
forward to greater heights and to a wider horizon than that which represented the mind-content of our progenitors...   Astrology Pages 144*

Thought Vibration or The Law of Attraction in the Thought World   ISBN: *1-59462-127-6*   **$12.95**
by William Walker Atkinson   Psychology/Religion Pages 144

Optimism *by Helen Keller*   ISBN: *1-59462-108-X*   **$15.95**
*Helen Keller was blind, deaf, and mute since 19 months old, yet famously learned how to overcome these handicaps, communicate with the world, and
spread her lectures promoting optimism. An inspiring read for everyone...   Biographies/Inspirational Pages 84*

Sara Crewe *by Frances Burnett*   ISBN: *1-59462-360-0*   **$9.45**
*In the first place, Miss Minchin lived in London. Her home was a large, dull, tall one, in a large, dull square, where all the houses were alike, and all the
sparrows were alike, and where all the door-knockers made the same heavy sound...   Childrens/Classic Pages 88*

The Autobiography of Benjamin Franklin *by Benjamin Franklin*   ISBN: *1-59462-135-7*   **$24.95**
*The Autobiography of Benjamin Franklin has probably been more extensively read than any other American historical work, and no other book of its kind
has had such ups and downs of fortune. Franklin lived for many years in England, where he was agent...   Biographies/History Pages 332*

Name	
Email	
Telephone	
Address	
City, State ZIP	

☐ **Credit Card**   ☐ **Check / Money Order**

Credit Card Number	
Expiration Date	
Signature	

Please Mail to: Book Jungle
PO Box 2226
Champaign, IL 61825
or Fax to: 630-214-0564

www.ingramcontent.com/pod-product-compliance
Lightning Source LLC
Chambersburg PA
CBHW080748250626
47162CB00010B/3064